Starscape

Starscape

The Silver Bullet

Brad Aiken

To Neil & Babe — Enjoy — Brad A.

Writers Club Press

New York   Lincoln   Shanghai

Starscape
The Silver Bullet

Copyright © 2000 by Bradley M Aiken
edited by Susan Cumins

Writers Club Press
an imprint of iUniverse, Inc.

iUniverse books may be ordered through booksellers or by contacting:

iUniverse
2021 Pine Lake Road, Suite 100
Lincoln, NE 68512
www.iuniverse.com
1-800-Authors (1-800-288-4677)

ISBN-13: 978-0-595-13548-6
ISBN-10: 0-595-13548-X

Printed in the United States of America

To Laura

Contents

CHAPTER I

The Western

The sand glistened as the morning sun poured over the mountains of the San Bernardino desert. The air was cool and crisp but Jesse knew it was going to be another typical sultry day in southern California. Today was his eighteenth birthday, and Jesse beamed with excitement in anticipation of the big day ahead. He would finally get to ride with the Dalton gang.

Jesse's dad, Harry Dalton, was a stately-appearing man of fifty-two years, and the streaks of gray that peered through his sideburns only served to enhance his image. He came to California looking for gold in the rush of 1849, but found only hardship. He had struggled for months just to feed his family and pay the inflated rent on the drafty hole of a shack that sheltered them. Young Jesse was strong, but his mother wasn't so lucky. Sally Dalton was a frail woman, but too kind to injure her husband's pride by letting him know how the conditions in which they were living were affecting her health. She showed no sign of the weakness eating away at her day after day, and Harry was devastated when she began to show the signs of the disease that was destroying her body from inside. She fought bravely, but gradually lost to the consumption. Life for Harry and Jesse would never be the same.

Determined to get his gold one way or another, and callused by the rude twist of fate that this beautiful new west had brought him, Harry gathered a group of friends soon to be renowned as The Dalton Gang. At first they were satisfied to loot gold from some of the luckier miners, but they quickly moved on to bigger things. They had become the scourge of the desert as they methodically went from town to town robbing the local banks. Harry was smart and kept the strikes unpredictable at first, but as the strikes got bigger, the number of possible targets got smaller. He looked with concerned pride as he watched his son saddling up the men's horses. He couldn't refuse young Jesse the ride he had been promising for years. But Harry Dalton knew that a posse would be waiting for them in Silver Creek.

Silver Creek was a small town at the edge of the desert. The creek that flowed from beautiful Palm Canyon into the town had never yielded an ounce of silver. In fact, no silver was ever found anywhere near Silver Creek. The town had changed its name from Palm Canyon to Silver Creek during the lean early years of the gold rush. People had flocked away, seeking their fortunes in other towns during those years, and the merchants of Palm Canyon were barely breaking even. In a stroke of genius, the town's mayor suggested the deceitful name of Silver Creek to draw the masses of fortune hunters through town. Deceit was sweet for Silver Creek. Silver never flowed, but the miners' money sure did. The merchants flourished and the town used its prosperity to develop farms and lucrative Silver Creek ranches. This was a wealthy town, and they knew it was just a matter of time before the Daltons would come. Silver Creek was waiting for Harry Dalton.

Jesse anxiously saddled the horses as he watched the men gather their gear. He knew his job, and he would have the horses ready to ride in plenty of time. The Dalton Gang had swelled to seventeen men and was a formidable group when geared up for a fight. Several of them had served in the cavalry before coming west to seek their fortunes. They weren't the lucky ones, and time had made them bitter. Harry Dalton gathered his men and set off for Silver Creek.

It was a typical Monday morning in the well-manicured streets of the Silver Creek business district. Shopkeepers were preparing to open up for the day as the sun began to warm the crisp morning air of springtime. The streets bustled with activity as Dalton's scouts rode into town. It was business as usual for the merchants of Silver Creek as the streets filled with activity. It was anything but obvious to Dalton's scouts that a thirty-man posse of sharpshooters was positioned along Main Street. The Gang would find their way in an easy ride, but the getaway would be another story.

Dalton felt uneasy as his scouts recounted the layout of Silver Creek. There had been no sign of recognition that the gang was on its way, and to Dalton this smelled like a trap. They had to make this strike, but Harry Dalton was too smart to go in blind. Five of his best men were already in Silver Creek paving the way for an escape through the canyon at the edge of town—a difficult route no one would anticipate. They backtracked and entered the bank at 11:45 A.M..

It was high noon when the gang rode in. Harry liked high noon; it was unbearably hot and the townspeople were generally indoors enjoying lunch. He always tried to catch a town with its guard down. They entered town in three groups to avert suspicion and converged simultaneously on the bank. As the twelve men watched the street, Dalton's five advance men were already inside securing the bank. There wasn't a sound and the men of the posse, who were anticipating a confrontation with an infamous group of fighters, were completely unaware that they were missing out on all the action. Dalton casually strode in the front door of the bank and gathered the money with his men. This was all too simple and he had an uneasy feeling in the pit of his stomach. He gave the signal and his men headed around back with the horses.

Sheriff Dodd was suspicious at the gathering of strangers in front of the bank, and when he saw them take the extra horses around back, he went to check things out. As the sheriff walked in, a shot resounded. Harry Dalton, smoking gun in his hand, stood motionless. He'd never shot anyone face to face before. His heists were always well planned to avoid confrontation. He didn't consider himself a man of violence.

"Come on, Harry," Bart Jenkins pleaded as he pulled the stunned Dalton away.

Dalton quickly snapped out of his momentary trance and dashed out back to mount his horse as the posse was responding to the commotion. He threw his body up onto the well-broken leather saddle and followed closely behind the rest of his men. The chase was on.

The gang's horses were the finest, but not as fresh as the horses of Silver Creek, and they struggled to stay ahead of the closing posse. Bullets were flying past their heads, and the sound of gunfire echoed through the valley as they turned out of town and negotiated the rough terrain of Palm Canyon. The horses' hooves pounded heavily into the hard dry clay, sending up a cloud of dust so thick that the posse's shots could only be aimed at the dirty haze enshrouding the gang. Jesse's eyes were tearing from the dry clay dust swarming all around him. He could see little more than the blur of horses that he followed, trailed only by his watchful father. He was terrified. *This ain't as much fun as I figured,* he thought, as a wave of panic swept over him. The Daltons were losing ground when suddenly there was a tremendous rumble and everything began to shake. No one reacted as the chase continued. There was a loud sonic blast as the earth shook again.

"What the hell?" Stryker muttered as he realized it wasn't the earth shaking, but the whole damned holovision set. This was one of his favorite westerns and he knew this didn't look right. "What the hell's going on here?" he shouted, as he spun in his chair and looked toward a man of Atlas-like proportions, his copilot, T.C. McGee.

"Switch to the rear viewer and hold on tight!" T.C. yelled, as a third blast shook the ship.

Stryker switched the screen to the rear viewer.

"A Teconean battle cruiser! What the hell are they doing here?"

The ship lurched forward.

"Correction," said T.C.. "What the hell were they doing *there*?"

The screen went blank and so did Stryker's stomach. "I hate that," he mumbled. He never could get used to hyperspatial travel.

"It's a good thing they haven't figured a way to put warp drive onto those big cruisers yet," quipped T.C..

"Yeah, maybe I should get one of those big babies," laughed Stryker.

CHAPTER II

Back Home

Danny Stryker was a tall slender man, a bit of a free spirit, but intense about everything he ever took on. He had been the pride of the Academy back in the 2480's—top academic honors, the best fighter-pilot, and not a woman's head he couldn't turn. All of the cadets envied Stryker; he was blessed with all the gifts. *All but one*, pondered Stryker as he soberly recalled those times of youth. *The one quality*, he thought, *that I couldn't be blessed with was diplomacy.* Danny always spoke his mind. No matter who said what, Danny always knew that he was right and didn't know how to be gracious about it. Funny thing was, everybody else knew Danny was right too, but it rubbed the top brass the wrong way, especially General Streight. *Not a good man to antagonize*, Danny reminisced, as he shook his head gently from side to side with memories so vivid he could feel them. General Streight was the Commander General in charge of Space Corps operations.

"Hey!" said T.C. to a dazed-looking Stryker. "You gonna join me here? I could use a little help bringing this baby down."

Stryker was lost in the past, but quickly snapped back to reality. He never thought he would return here to Omnicenter. He swore he'd never come back, but when Omnicenter Command called in every available pilot, even him and T.C., Danny knew that things had reached the point of no return.

"Thinking about her again, aren't you?" piped in T.C..

"Believe it or not, no," Danny said, to his own amazement.

'Her' was Major Jennifer Lee, a dazzling black-haired beauty who had stolen Danny's heart. Hardly a day went by that he hadn't thought of her since he had left the Space Corps. She had been a freshman new to the Academy in Danny's junior year, and became the envy of every woman there when she caught Danny's eye. Everyone including Danny knew that they would marry. Everyone, that is, except for Jennifer. Although she was in love with Danny, she was determined to pursue her career dreams. By the middle of her senior year, she had accepted a science post at Omnicenter that would commence upon her matriculation, an assignment that would not allow her to travel with a Space Corps captain for the long periods of time he would be away from Earth. After she accepted the post, Danny was never the same. He stayed with the Space Corps long enough to win major accolades and become the youngest Space Corps captain in history. But the day she began her job at Omnicenter, reality hit home for Danny. His patience shortened, and he could no longer control his intolerance for the rigidity of the Space Corps. That was the beginning of the end of his career as a Space Corps officer.

"Yo, Danny. You gonna give me a hand here?" quipped T.C. as Danny stared blankly ahead.

"Now I am thinking about her. Thanks a lot."

"Sorry about that, Danny, but too late to think about it now."

They were making their final approach to the Omnicenter spaceport. Omnicenter was the greatest city in Federation territory. It had developed on the African Continent of Earth back in the twenty-second century. By the time that Earth had finally advanced enough to develop uniform global systems of government and commerce, which would become known as the Federation, Africa was one of the few continents that had room to bring to fruition the concept of Omnicenter—a huge city developed solely to serve as home base for the Federation Command Center. This is where the Academy was established and where diplomats and military alike from all over the Federation relocated their families to develop a unified center for all of the Federation affairs. It was the hub of technological advancement, and throughout the exploration and settlement of the Federation's outworlds, it remained the center for commerce, politics and the unified military branch of the Federation—the Space Corps. By the twenty-fifth century, there were thirteen planets in the Federation. Earth was the closest to the Teconean planets, and the remainder of the twelve Federation worlds fanned out from Earth away from Teconean space.

Danny and T.C. were awestruck. Omnicenter had doubled in size since they had last seen it. The glitter of steel and glass stretched out as far as the eye could see. But what frightened them was the hoard of ships in port and the chaotic activity with which the port bustled. Things were normally very orderly at Omnicenter. Order was the way, and order was the reason that Danny couldn't stay. But the stifling regimented lifestyle that Stryker remembered had been replaced by masses of people scurrying in apparently aimless patterns. Stryker and McGee had docked and an escort awaited them.

General Alexander Thompson was a dignified-looking man of African American descent. His large, powerful physique was intimidating, but his warm manner melted away the gruff exterior every time he shook someone's hand and began to speak. Stryker had had his differences with Thompson but remembered him with warm respect. Thompson had risen through the ranks quickly and, at the age of forty-five, he had been second in command at the Space Corps when Stryker graduated. Two years later, when General Streight died in a warp core meltdown aboard the Galaxy I, Thompson was appointed Commander General of the Space Corps. He was the youngest commander general in Federation history and brought with him a vibrant resurgence of creativity, long stifled by Streight's rigid leadership style. When Danny had heard about the change, he had thoughts of returning to the Space Corps, but the memories were too painful and he had already developed a successful career as a trader that he was not anxious to give up for the restrictive life of the military.

Thompson admired Stryker's brash style and was one of the few who backed him up when Stryker was bucking the system. When Stryker made his decision to leave the Corps, Thompson was distraught but he understood. He knew that the Space Corps couldn't afford to lose a man like Danny Stryker, but he also realized why Danny couldn't stay.

"It's good to see you, Captain Stryker," said Thompson as he extended his hand.

"You too, sir. But you know very well that I left that 'Captain' title far behind me."

The general looked him straight in the eyes. "To me, Danny, you will always be an officer of the Corps. God knows, if anyone deserves that honor, you do." Alexander Thompson was generally the epitome of self-assurance. It looked strange to see the fear in his face as he uncharacteristically glanced briefly down at the ground, then again met Danny's gaze. "We need your help."

An icy chill swept through Danny's body and he paled with anticipation of the unwanted news.

Thompson led Stryker and McGee into the rear chamber of his spacious office and slid open a hidden panel in the wall on the far side of the chamber. As the wall slipped open, the heart of the Omnicenter defense system came into plain view. They stood at the entrance to a large chamber with intergalactic maps and statistical display stations, which formed a ring around the center of the room. A single officer was studying the instruments. He turned as they walked in.

"Ski!" Danny started, "I thought that you were…"

"Dead?" Captain Kolanski finished the sentence.

Steven Kolanski had been an all-honors student. A mathematical whiz, he had finished second in his class at the Academy. But being second to Danny Stryker was an honor for Ski. He had been Danny's only true friend in those days. That is, until he left to fight in a border skirmish with Teconean scout ships the day after graduation. He never came back, and the final thread that had held Danny to Omnicenter was gone, clearing the way for him to leave when he finally got too fed up with the bureaucracy.

"My ship wrecked and I was stranded on Antari IV for almost two years. By the time I got back here, you were gone. They told me that you had left a few days earlier. For six months I tried to track you down; I finally gave up. I felt kind of betrayed. Where the hell were you?"

Danny felt sick. He had gotten messages from Omnicenter, but never dreamed they were from Ski. He never answered those messages and never looked back.

"Everywhere," said Danny, "looking for anything and finding nothing." He strode over to Kolanski and gave him a hearty embrace.

Thompson's stolid voice interrupted the brief reunion. "Ski will fill you in."

"You know we've been at odds with the Teconean Empire for some time. But what you may not know is that things are heating up."

Danny knew all too well how hot things had become from the unpleasant encounter he and T.C. had had with the Teconean cruiser just one day earlier, as they were passing through the abandoned Orion solar system.

"Nothing has been said, but we've detected mass movements of Teconean cruisers in the past three weeks. We believe that they may finally be preparing for the assault they've been threatening for years. They must believe that they now have the capability to crush the Federation, though we're not sure where their confidence comes from. We know of course of their increasing numbers of cruisers, but they've never had the technology to network their fleet into a coordinated attack force or to set up adequate defense systems for the planets of the Empire. It would take some sort of massive tech center, likely located within the Teconean system. If they have managed this, we're doomed. We surely cannot match their numbers. As you know, they've poured most of their resources into military development over the past century. We've always relied on our technological edge to maintain peace. And if this techno-center of theirs exists, it's well hidden. Space Corps Command has scanned every likely area and come up dry each time. I can only hope that it does not exist."

"It does," said Danny dryly.

Thompson, Ski and T.C. all stared at Danny in fearful apprehension. They knew that his hunches were never wrong.

"And I know where it is."

The room was silent. Everyone stared at Stryker and a look of curiosity crept across the face of T.C. McGee, who had been with Stryker continuously for months. Stryker had never mentioned a word of this to him before.

"You wanna let me in on this, buddy?"

"We were there yesterday," replied Danny.

"Of course," T.C. muttered with a nod. "The battle cruiser."

Stryker explained the encounter that he and T.C. had had with the Teconean cruiser the day before to Thompson and Ski. He realized that no Teconean ship would dare risk attacking a Federation ship in times of peace. The Federation was too technologically advanced and the Teconean command too fearful of retaliation. Yet the Teconean fleet had attacked their ship. The only possible explanation was that Danny and T.C. must have stumbled too close to an area that was so sensitive that the Teconean Command was willing to risk retaliation to try and blow Stryker's ship off the map. It all made sense now—the Teconean technocenter did exist, and it was in the Orion system.

The Orion star system was the site of the planet Tri-Luna, a beautiful planet named for its three moons. It had been the first real attempt at establishing a human settlement on another planet. Chosen largely for its proximity to Earth, it met only the barest requirements for human colonization—a breathable environment with adequate oxygen and acceptable levels of other gases, a small star that it circled to provide enough warmth to barely take the edge off of the frosty year-round breezes, a copious supply of water, and an adequate but exhausting gravitational pull, which at 1.2 g's took its toll on even the hardiest of the early settlers. It was the combination of the cold, thin air and the 1.2 g's that deterred civilian settlement and eventually caused explorers to abandon the Orion system once more distant, and more desirable, systems became accessible through the advancement of hyperspatial travel.

It all made perfect sense now. A Teconean technocenter within close proximity to the heart of the Federation, yet hidden in an area ignored by the Federation for centuries, and blanketed in ion storms that shielded it from long-range sensors. It was obviously not operational yet, or the attack would have surely begun, but it was clear that time was limited.

Stryker didn't like what was developing. Even in times of peace he wanted nothing to do with the Space Corps. He certainly did not want to fight their wars.

"As you saw when you arrived in Omnicenter, we've called in every available pilot with combat experience," said Thompson.

"Yeah, we saw the chaos. So what do you need me for?" snapped Stryker. "This place is crawling with fighter pilots—most of them a lot younger and more eager than I am."

The magnetic gaze of Alexander Thompson caught Stryker's eyes. "None with your strategic skills. You're the best, Stryker, the best I've ever known."

"Gee, Chief. You're gonna make me blush."

This was quite a compliment from a man not known for flattery, a man who built his reputation for speaking his peace. But he, unlike Stryker, knew when to keep quiet; he never said a word that was not logically thought out and sincere.

"Damn it," Stryker mumbled to himself. He knew there would be no life for him to live if the Teconean Command destroyed the Federation.

"I don't know," muttered Danny, knowing full well that he was in it to stay.

Thompson knew it too. "We need to buy some time."

"For what?" asked Danny, his interest piqued.

"Come with me. There is something I have to show you."

Thompson pointed as he led the way. He guided the group down a long passageway lighted by the unmistakable greenish glow of phosphor walls. There weren't many windows in the heart of Omnicenter, partially for protection and partially for the lack of anything to look at other than the metallic structures, all crammed together to maximize usable space in this oldest section of the city. Phosphor-impregnated walls lighted most access areas in Omnicenter these days. As Ski punched in the pass code to enter the Space Corps' research and development lab, Thompson began to explain.

"We've known for some time of our vulnerability to the Teconean forces, should they develop a technocenter capable of monitoring and unifying their fleet the way we developed Omnicenter Central back in the twenty-second century."

The doors slipped open silently, and the four men entered the vestibule that led to the main corridor of the R & D lab. "Seven years ago," Thompson continued, "our scientists began working on a solution. This solution was to be the ultimate defense weapon, the FDS, or Federation Defense System. The device was to have the capability to neutralize any energy source passing through a zone surrounding it. On a planetary scale, the FDS power field would be like the rings of Saturn, but in the shape of a sphere, and with the ability to de-energize any ambient power source attempting to pass through it. By creating this field, which would have no effect at its center in order to spare the location and energy supply of the device itself, our planets would be impregnable to any energy-based device as we know it. What's more, by outfitting our ships with these devices, they could enter any battle or any Teconean zone without fear of destruction."

"Incredible," gasped T.C..

"Amen," agreed Stryker. "Then what in the heck do you need us for?"

Ski got ready to speak but Thompson interjected. "As I said, Captain, we need to buy some time. Our scientists are close, but the device is not yet operational. The design of the critical central core stabilizer control has eluded them thus far. I'm not a scientist, so I don't understand all of the technicalities, but it has something to do with the stabilization of the center of the energy field. As the FDS field is generated, a null central core must be created in order to negate the effect of the field on its user, otherwise everything on the planet would lose power, including the FDS itself."

Thompson paused as he noticed the vacuous look in Danny's and T.C.'s eyes. "Not too clear, huh? I told you I didn't really understand all of this stuff." He looked up in thought. "Let's see, how did Quigley explain this to me?"

"Let me try," broke in Kolanski. "Listen, guys, think of the FDS like a giant egg. Earth is the egg yolk. The FDS energy field surrounds Earth, just like the shell surrounds the egg yolk. And just like the shell protects the egg yolk, the FDS field protects Earth—it won't allow harmful things to penetrate and get to the yolk. Got it?"

They shook their heads in unison.

"Good, O.K. then," Ski continued. "Now, in the egg, the only layer of protection is the hard shell, and in the FDS the only layer of protection is the outer energy field—picture it like a thin shell of energy surrounding Earth. And between Earth and the outer energy field, the shell, is a buffer zone, like the egg white. This buffer zone protects Earth from being harmed by the energy field of the FDS, like the egg white keeps the yolk from bumping against the shell. You with me?"

"Yeah, keep going."

"Now comes the tricky part. Unlike the eggshell, the FDS energy field is dynamic, always in motion, so the protective buffer zone between the shell and Earth must also be dynamic. In order to keep the fields stable, a dynamic phase controller has to be employed to insure a perfect phase match. In other words, the phase of the buffer zone has to constantly be adjusted to keep it in sync with the phase of the outer energy field or the FDS is worthless."

"In fact," interrupted Thompson, "worse than that, it can destabilize the central core so forcefully that it could rip apart the planet on which it is activated."

Danny looked surprised. "Why risk doing it on Earth then?"

"He tends to be a bit dramatic," broke in Kolanski. "It's really not dangerous the way it's been designed. There are so many safeguards that it will shut itself down at the first inkling of a malfunction. Omnicenter is the ideal place for the prototype. After all, we're going to be the prime target if the Empire ever gets bold enough to attack. That's a far greater risk than the FDS."

"Sounds like the arguments used by the United States and Russia during the nuclear arms race," said Danny.

"The what?" said Ski with a puzzled look.

"Man! Did you sleep through all of your history classes?"

"Who didn't! Professor Pistanskiewicz was the biggest bore we had. You mean you really remember that stuff?"

"Are you with me, gentlemen?" Thompson interrupted.

The two old classmates looked at each other and laughed. "Right here," Danny said.

They had reached the end of a long corridor and entered the main R&D lab. As they passed into the anteroom, they were in a glass-enclosed chamber. A strange tingling sensation flashed briefly through them, subtle but unmistakable to anyone who had ever experienced it.

"I always hated that," T.C. said. "No matter how many times I go through that static neutralizer, I'll never get used to it."

They moved on to a changing area where they were given cleansuits to wear, then on to another glass-enclosed room for suction treatment to remove any remaining traces of dust.

They were now prepared to enter the outer lab area. A large panel slid open and allowed the group to pass into a huge chamber, brilliantly lit but softened by the uniformly tinted ice-blue walls visible throughout the maze of glass-enclosed rooms which surrounded them. The main corridors were highlighted with luminescent dark blue edge-molding, which stood out clearly but unobtrusively from the ambient pale blue light. These smaller glass-enclosed rooms were where the actual microtech work took place. Each corridor had its own anteroom where a final decontamination process took place before anyone could enter. The inner chambers were spotless, dust-free, static-free, and air-free. The scientists within wore pressurized suits to protect them from the vacuum environment of their labs. Ski led them down the main corridor to a group of clandestine research rooms which were not apparent from the main entry chamber, as their pale blue walls blended in with the surrounding light. He entered his code, allowing the doors to open upon recognition of his voice pattern as he stated his name and title. The room was physically isolated by opaque, soundproof walls which yielded an eerie silence as the door slid closed behind them.

Dr. Quigley looked up when he saw them approaching. Stryker recognized the professor as any Academy alumnus would. Quigley was the foremost research scientist of the modern era, and had become Omnicenter's top scientist by the age of thirty-three. It came as no surprise to Stryker that he was heading the project.

Thompson pointed to the center of the room where a very distinctive structure was located. It was a small metallic obelisk 0.25 meters in height with a strange iridescence and black diamond-shaped notches every two centimeters marching up the length of each side.

"That," said Thompson, "is the heart of the FDS central core stabilizer."

Danny Stryker had the most curious expression on his face that T.C. had ever seen, and it made him nervous. Thompson noticed too.

"What's the matter, Stryker?"

Danny stood in silence.

"Just warp lag," T.C. broke in hopefully, fearing what might really be going on in Danny's mind.

"Right," Danny said, "I guess that's it."

Doubtingly, Thompson nodded. He knew that there was more to this, but he also knew that there was no point in pursuing it. He knew that Danny would tell him what was on his mind only when Danny was ready.

"Ski will see you out, gentlemen. The pilots' briefing is at 0800 hours tomorrow. See you then."

Chapter III

The Good Old Days

In spite of the intergalactic standard calendar that had been adopted to unify the worlds of the Federation, many of those on Earth enjoyed using the old Earth time standard to avoid anonymity and maintain a connection with what they considered the most romantic heritage in the galaxy. The tales of ancient Earth history had most certainly become twisted through the years, with imprecise recounting of the glorious times of ancient civilizations, of pharaohs and gods, of the parting of the seas and the slaying of dragons, of kings and knights and pirates' lore. Each man and woman who could lay claim to having grown from these roots had his or her favorite tales. It was the idyllic escape from a humanity so intertwined with technology that many could no longer distinguish the two. A flight into fantasies of the past often rekindle the spark of individuality that every human being needs to feel now and then, to remind them of their worth. Even renegades like Danny Stryker needed to delve into fantasy once in a while; especially renegades like Danny Stryker, whose distaste of an overly bureaucratic society was what made them renegades in the first place. Like everyone else, Danny had his favorite time period, the North American "Old West."

Stryker was silent all the way back to the ship.

"I can't stand it anymore," said T.C. as they entered the cabin.

"What? Did you say something, buddy?" muttered Stryker as he continued to stare blindly ahead.

"Danny, what's going through that head of yours? You're making me nervous!"

Danny walked into his chambers without saying a word.

I guess he's finally flipped, thought T.C.. "Coming back here really got to you, didn't it, man?"

The door shut behind Stryker automatically, and T.C. followed him in. "I've known you too long, Danny. I'm not going to turn my back and watch you do it again," he shouted, thinking back to Danny's torrid exit from the Space Corps after Jennifer had jilted him.

Danny hadn't heard a word that T.C. had said. When he entered his chambers he headed straight for his book compartment. He had taken a lot of ribbing for his fascination with Earth's early western American history, or the Old West, as Stryker liked to call it, keeping with tradition. He had the best collection of early American non-fiction and fiction books in existence, having spent most of his precious free time at the Academy scavenging the planet for the old memorabilia. He was flipping through the fading pages of the pride of his collection, *The Life and Times of Billy Delaney*, when T.C. walked into the room.

"I'll be damned," he whispered, as he looked up at T.C. for the first time since they had left Space Corps headquarters. He gazed in amazement as he pointed out a yellowed picture. T.C. looked down and his jaw dropped so wide open that a bird could have landed in there. "I never knew for sure whether this book was fact or fiction before, but I guess this cinches it."

There on the faded yellow page was a photograph of Billy Delaney and a motley looking crew, with a sign overhead reading "Wild West Show," and there at the center of the sign, resting atop a high post, was a gleaming obelisk with small black diamond-shaped markings along the side facing the camera. It had always looked somehow out of place to Danny, its perfect symmetry and polished reflection standing out in sharp contrast to everything else in the picture. This photo had always fascinated him.

"You don't suppose it could be a coincidence, do you?"

"I sure hope so," replied T.C., still staring at the photo.

It was unmistakably the same obelisk that was sitting in the Space Corps' lab. The same top-secret project that no one outside of Omnicenter had ever seen, much less heard of.

"What the hell's going on here?" Stryker muttered.

He didn't sleep well that night. There were only two possible explanations for the picture in Billy Delaney's book: either Quigley shared Danny's fascination with the Old West and had decided to model his FDS project after an old photo (*Not likely*, Danny thought. *That lovable old coot wouldn't be interested in anything that happened before the computer age.*), or the obelisk somehow was sent back in time to the Life and Times of Billy Delaney—a frightening thought, but it seemed the only answer.

The thought haunted Stryker all night. He couldn't help but wonder how the obelisk could have gotten into the hands of Billy Delaney, and more importantly, *when* it got there. Danny had heard the rumors that the Space Corps was working on a time-warp system, but had never taken them very seriously. After all, the human race had been fascinated with the idea of time travel since the concept of time was first developed. If the time-warp system was in fact perfected, and the obelisk had been sent back in its unfinished, nonfunctional form, it wouldn't make much difference, but if it had been sent back after Quigley had perfected it, then Billy Delaney's obelisk could be the final product—the key to defeating the Teconean Empire. Danny's head was spinning.

CHAPTER IV

Back to the Chief

It was a crisp, clear morning, the kind of day that made Alexander Thompson long for the time when cities had been open to the atmosphere. He ached to go outside and feel the cool breezes of Fall against his face, but he didn't have the time it would take to make his way to the nearest exit port. Even the thought of having to obtain clearance at one of the government-controlled ports killed the joy of his reminiscences. As he came to the entrance of the Space Corps Command Center, his head was still in the clouds. He reached out to slip his keycard into the door lock and a tap on the shoulder startled him.

"You workin' half days in your old age, General? It's almost 0800!" Danny Stryker had been standing near the entrance waiting for him.

"I was hoping to bring you over to my side, Danny, but I didn't think you'd give in quite so fast. I'm afraid to ask you this, but what convinced you? I've got a feeling that it's trouble."

"After you, sir," Danny said, holding the door open.

An alarm sounded as they came through the main entranceway, and an impersonal, computer-generated voice warned, "Please step aside, Captain Stryker, and place your belongings on the inspection table." Danny shot a curious glance at Thompson.

"I took the liberty of obtaining clearance and reinstating you in Command Center's computer banks," Thompson explained to Danny.

"A bit cocky, weren't you, General?" Danny retorted. "I didn't think I was that easy."

"This object does not meet Space Corps Command's clearance codes for entrance into Command Center, Captain," came the analytical admonition from the robotic security guard, as it lifted the fragile, yellowed edition of The *Life and Times of Billy Delaney*.

"Hey, you tin lizzy! Be careful with that thing, it's more fragile than your flimsy little processor, and a heck of a lot more valuable."

"Is there a problem here, sir?" asked an authoritative voice from the chief of security, as the human guards approached the inspection station.

"What is that old thing, Stryker?" inquired General Thompson. "You know the rules about bringing uncataloged objects in here that the security computer can't identify."

Stryker pulled the general aside. "*That* is why I was here so early," he whispered as he motioned in the direction of the old book. "I think we'd better continue this discussion in your office, sir."

General Thompson turned back to the security chief. "I'll take the responsibility for this, Chief."

The security chief recognized General Thompson and knew better than to question his authority. Both men were quiet as they made their way back into the command section of the Omnicenter, and headed up the passageway to the general's office. Thompson knew Stryker, and he knew that Danny wouldn't have broken regulations if he didn't have something big up his sleeve. As they approached the door to Thompson's office, another artificial voice broke in, but this voice was soft and feminine, unlike the harsh tones of the security computer.

"Please identify yourself."

The voice had a warm, almost seductive, tone, but Thompson was very prompt and professional in his response, as always. If the right response to the deceptively benign voice hadn't been relayed within five seconds, everyone in the corridor would have be stunned senseless, giving the security force time to arrive.

"Thompson, Alexander," was the terse reply. The door slid open.

Inside was a vast chamber loaded with the most sophisticated intelligence gathering equipment in the Federation. Stryker had only guessed at the appearance of these chambers before. He had never been privy to their contents.

"Come on in, Stryker. Let's talk."

Stryker had always felt that Thompson was one of the few men who had treated him fairly, but he now knew the deep sense of trust that the general held for him. Few men ever entered these chambers.

They made their way across the brightly-lit room and past the smoked-glass desk that was inlaid with numerous infoscreens, the braincenter of the commander general's office. Thompson led him through a small doorway, into a warmly-lit room with antique sofas and chairs that looked as if they dated back to twentieth-century America. There was a strange, yellow-hued light illuminating the room, and the walls were uncharacteristically dark, without a trace of the all-too-familiar phosphor glow that impregnated nearly every wall in the city. Danny spotted the source of the light.

"I've read about those in my old books," he remarked as he studied the strange objects that lit the room. They were cylindrical glass vases with cloth-covered shades at the top concealing small glowing bulbs beneath. "I think they called them incandescent lamps, didn't they?" he asked as he reached his hand in toward the light. "Ouch!" he shrieked, jumping back and putting his painful finger to his mouth.

"Authentic down to the inefficient heat-emitting light bulb," laughed Thompson. "Now make yourself comfortable and tell me what you've got," he said with a more characteristically serious tone in his voice.

Stryker eased down uncomfortably into one of the two plush leather recliners that were positioned on either side of a mahogany lamp table. Thompson, already seated in the adjacent chair, was watching Stryker and could sense his disquieting demeanor. Stryker slid forward on his seat and laid the old book between them on the table. Without saying a word he flipped open the book to expose the picture of the Wild West

Show and the eye-catching obelisk. Thompson glanced curiously over at Stryker as he leaned forward to look at the book.

"What could possibly be so important in this old piece of junk that you…good God!" he gasped as he saw the picture. "Where did this picture come from? This is a top secret project." The general paled as he slumped back into his chair.

"It came from 1849," Danny said quietly. "I know my American Old West history. This book—and this picture—are authentic. I was never sure if it was fact or fiction, but I had this book carbondated and I know for sure that it was published in the 1800s."

The two men sat and alternately stared at each other, then at the book, then back at each other for what seemed like an eternity.

"This all makes no sense, Danny," said Thompson calmly in an informal tone that was so out of character that Stryker knew his commander was caught as off guard as he was and, more importantly, that he believed him.

"I've been over and over this in my head, sir, and there are only two possible explanations. The first is highly unlikely, and the second…" Danny paused and the general met his gaze. "The second is too frightening to think about."

Danny elaborated on his two theories, and the general reluctantly agreed that these were the only possible explanations. It would be easy enough to check with Quigley to exclude the unlikely possibility that he had modeled the obelisk after an old picture, and the two men were already on their way to talk with the professor. Both men were ominously quiet as they made their way down the winding corridors. They both realized that if the fully-operational obelisk had been taken back in time, then the universe as they knew it could cease to exist at any moment. If the people who came into possession of the obelisk ever stumbled on its powers, the entire course of the history of intergalactic colonization and development could be changed, and it would be as if the world that Stryker and Thompson lived in had never existed at all.

The two men approached the entrance to the Research & Development Lab and Thompson broke the eerie silence as he addressed the computer security system.

"Thompson, Alexander. Request immediate council with Dr. Quigley. Code One. Priority One."

After a few brief seconds, the mechanical reply came. "Please proceed directly to Lab Central offices. Dr. Quigley will await you there. Have a nice day."

"If you only knew the half of it," Stryker muttered to the security computer as they turned away.

The two men met a rather nervous Professor Quigley as they approached his office. Quigley had *never* been sought for a priority one emergency, and his sense of near panic was clear.

"Relax, Professor," Danny said as they met. Stryker's air of perpetual self-confidence always had a calming effect on those around him.

Quigley seemed to gradually feel more at ease as they made their way into his office. "You really had me worried there," he said to the men, with a sigh of relief.

"You should be," Thompson said somberly, and Quigley's anxiety immediately resurfaced.

Stryker pulled out the book and went through the whole explanation again with Quigley. Much to their chagrin, Quigley gave them the response they had anticipated: he had never seen the picture before. The design of the obelisk originated from very precise scientific calculations.

"Who else knows about this, Danny?" the general asked, as both men looked Stryker's way.

"Just me, you two and T.C., far as I know. I doubt that another copy of this book even exists, and this one's been in my quarters ever since I moved out of my folks' house to join the Academy."

Danny put in an emergency call to T.C. on the telecom, but there was no response. The three men headed anxiously back to Thompson's office to make some decisions. As they approached the office, they spotted T.C. pacing the corridor.

"Damn security computer wouldn't even patch me through to your office to see if you were in, General. I've been waiting here all morning to see if you would show up," T.C. said, and then looked right at his partner. "I didn't know where else to check, Danny. The way you stormed out of the ship this morning, I figured you'd be headed straight here. What in the hell's goin' on?"

"Come with us, Captain," Thompson said sternly. "I apologize for the security computer, but that's a primary protection system. They never give the location of any officers without appropriate pass code identification. I'll make sure you and Stryker are issued proper I.D. stat."

"*If* we join up, you mean," T.C. quipped.

"We just did," said Stryker.

T.C. shot a questioning glance at Stryker. He knew there would have to be something of major importance developing to make Danny rejoin the Space Corps so quickly.

Inside the general's office, the four men settled in without a word passing between them. Clearly this discussion was not going to be held in the quaint chambers the two men had left a short time ago, and they all followed the general into the heart of the main chamber. They took their places around the large smoked-glass Command Center desk, and all eyes were focused on General Thompson.

"Will somebody please tell me what's going on here?" T.C. demanded angrily. "Is this all about that dusty old picture you pulled out last night, man?"

Stryker nodded affirmatively and prepared to fill in his partner, but before he could say a word, Thompson broke in. "The time-warp system exists. Quigley made the breakthrough himself last July. It's operational and has been in use for a little over a year."

Stryker and T.C. gazed incredulously at Thompson, and slumped introspectively back into their chairs. After what seemed an eternity, Danny leaned forward and turned toward Thompson.

"I don't like it...I *really* don't like it, Danny," the general broke in before Stryker could open his mouth, "but I agree that it seems to be the only way."

General Thompson had anticipated Danny's thoughts. "I can arrange to obtain approval to equip a ship with time-warp drive, but it'll take some doing. Report back here at 0800 tomorrow and we'll start discussing tactical plans."

"Whoa, hold on there a minute!" protested T.C.. "I don't think I like the flow of this conversation. Any fool can see that you guys are planning on going back after that thing Danny saw in that old picture in the cowboy book, but this *isn't* some old Cowboys and Indians movie, this is reality, man. First off, *assuming* that this time-warp even works, which I'm not too thrilled about trying, by the way, and *assuming* that we could even find that Billy Delaney fellow who's got the obelisk, how do we know that it's the real thing? And even if it *is* Quigley's gadget, how do we know that it'll do us any good? That thing may be no more operational than the one sitting in the lab. Besides which, where do you get off sending Danny and me on this little leisure cruise? I'm not even sure I want to be in on any of this yet."

Danny patiently let his friend finish, and then began to answer before Thompson could finish gathering his thoughts. "It almost certainly *is* Quigley's gadget. The marks are quite distinctive, although we won't know for sure until we get our hands on it. If it is, then odds are that it will be operational, or at least closer to it than whatever we have now. You see, we know that the obelisk sitting in Quigley's lab is the only one in existence and has never been stolen. Therefore, the one that got into Billy Delaney's hands must have been taken back to him at some time in *our* future. In fact, since not too many people can get to Quigley's unit, it would figure to be some time after the obelisk is being mass produced for the Space Corps' ships. And at that point the units will be operational."

"It makes sense when you put it that way, Danny," T.C. said hesitantly, "but why us, Danny? Yesterday you didn't want to even be here, and today you're ready to go warping back in time, chasing a hunch to try and save the same Space Corps that stabbed you in the back."

"It has to be us,…or at least me, anyway," said Danny. "Lifestyles have changed a little in the last 650 years, and it's going to be damned near impossible for a Space Corps officer to fit in back in Billy Delaney's time. I'm the only one who knows enough about those days to have a chance of accomplishing this mission. And as for helping out the Space Corps, how would you like living under Teconean rule, pal?"

"Amazing," piped in Thompson. "You've figured out in one day what no one here would have come up with until we were under Teconean rule. It sure is nice to have you back, Danny."

General Thompson's eyes uncharacteristically turned toward the floor. "There is something else that you should know before you come in to be briefed on the time-warp drive tomorrow. The project is now under the direction of one of Quigley's top aides," he paused and took a deep breath, "Dr. Jennifer Lee."

Danny's self-assured expression vanished instantly, and his eyes darted up toward Thompson as if he was seeking reassurance that he had not heard correctly. Thompson's eyes were still fixed on the floor in front of him, and Danny's heart dropped to his knees.

Danny did not sleep well that night.

CHAPTER V

Time-warp

Jennifer Lee was a petite woman with dazzling beauty. Her fine facial features and shimmering long dark hair alluded to her Asian ancestry. She had taken a post at Omnicenter back in 2486 to the dismay of Danny Stryker and all their friends who were sure they would marry. It was a commitment that would not allow her the freedom to travel with Danny or give him the time it would take to make a marriage successful. She and Danny both knew that once she had made her decision, they had no future together. She was too much of a perfectionist to compromise either her career or her marriage for the other, and Danny certainly would not settle into an academic life—the only option that could keep him at Omnicenter full time. They both knew that Danny was no desk jockey. Once Jennifer had made her decision, she had also unwittingly changed the direction of Danny's life. He was never the same man after her fateful decision. His intolerance for the formalities of the system increased geometrically, and by the time she had graduated he knew that he could not continue to tolerate a life in the Space Corps.

Over the years that followed, Jennifer had thought of Danny as much as he had reflected on thoughts of her. Both of them denied these feelings adamantly, but it was plain to anyone who was close to either of them. She had been briefed about Danny's impending visit and was ready for his arrival at the lab. She had slept no better than he did the night before, but was determined not to let it show when Danny walked through the door.

Danny was up early that morning and took the long way to Omnicenter Command. He had always enjoyed a brisk walk through the cool crisp morning air. Predictably, the walk was a silent one. Virtually no one ventured out of doors on workdays anymore; it was much too time consuming. A robin flew by Danny's head and startled him. Not too many birds, or any wildlife for that matter, had survived the technological revolution on Earth outside of wildlife reserves (*Except the cockroaches!* Danny thought). He stared up in awe at the natural ease of the bird's flight; a few seemingly effortless strokes of the finely feathered wings lofted the robin high above his head, and then suspended motionless in the air, it glided swiftly away. Danny Stryker was still awed by the art of flight, something that few among the human race had mastered as well as he, and that no one respected more. There were few who appreciated flight as more than a science, and thus few who had achieved the piloting skills that Danny had.

His brisk walk ended at the entrance to Omnicenter Command. He hesitantly ambled through the hallways toward his meeting with Jennifer, and checked his watch as he approached her office. He did not wish to appear anxiously early. At 8:01 Danny knocked soundly at the door, feeling a false bravado. The door swung open and he entered quietly. His heart swelled in his chest as he saw the long dark hair of Jennifer Lee flowing down the back of her metallic-appearing uniform. The skin-tight, shimmering blue fiber of the outfit accentuated her petite sensual figure, and the silver accent which plunged from the sides of the uniform to meet at the small of her back just below the waistline created an unnecessary illusion. Jennifer, unlike less fortunate women, had no need to disguise the appearance of her already-narrow waist.

Slowly she turned toward him, determined to offer a nonchalant greeting, but as their eyes met, neither one of them could utter a word.

They both blushed as she broke the silence. "Shall we get to work, Captain?"

Her cool, businesslike greeting gave them both the strength they were searching for in an effort to deny their emotions.

"You lead the way, doc," he replied, and as she turned away he followed her into her lab.

She activated the computer and turned toward Danny. As her eyes met his in the closeness of the lab room, their defenses dropped.

"How've you been, Jen?"

"I missed you, Danny. I thought the pain was gone, but it's still not easy. I think we'd better stick to business. Please don't prey on my emotions, there isn't time."

"I think you've got things a little twisted around, Jen. You're the one who…"

A cold chill seemed to fill the air as they both turned toward the doorway. A tall muscular figure of a man stood in the doorway.

"I believe you know Captain Beck, Danny."

Hans Beck was an average student in his days at the Academy, he was nonetheless one of the more renowned students from Danny Stryker's class. His flying prowess was now legendary, and back in the Academy days, no one could come near matching his skill except Danny. Hans Beck had resented Danny for his academic brilliance and charismatic charm, two features that eluded this brash young pilot whose father had groomed him for the Academy since boyhood. Stryker had always enjoyed the competition in flight simulation tests, but to Beck it meant everything to be the best, and he usually won. In graduation competition, with all eyes on the two aces, Beck's hugely inflated ego hung in the balance as Danny Stryker put on an amazing display of spacemanship. When the bubble that was Hans Beck's ego had been burst, he felt a naked embarrassment for which he never forgave Danny Stryker.

As he entered the room, his cold stare bared his feelings in spite of his casual demeanor.

"I asked him to join us for this meeting," Jennifer said with a wry smile. "He's the only pilot who's used the time-warp system, and in light of the urgency of your mission, he'll be accompanying you."

Danny was not surprised. Beck's flying skills had made him the Space Corps' top test pilot, and Danny had heard of his daring successes. Nevertheless, he was not too thrilled with the idea of having this egotistical boar along for the ride.

"I wasn't planning on company for this trip, Dr. Lee."

"There's little time for discussion on the matter, Captain Stryker," she replied dryly. "Come with me."

She led him over to the holoemitter on her desk and called up the educational information on the newly-developed time-warp system.

"As you know the theory behind space-warp is quite simple, a matter of traveling from one point in space to another by warping, or spoken more plainly, bending the line that connects those two points until they are next to one another. It is then simply a matter of 'jumping' from one point to the other in a fraction of the time it would have taken to travel the distance without warping the space in between."

"Space physics 101," quipped Danny. "Any first year cadet knows that theory. I thought you said we were short on time."

"Precisely, Captain. That's why I'll expect no more interruptions."

She turned back to the holoemitter and continued, referring to the trimential pictures displayed above it. A three-dimensional visualization of the time-warp theory unfolded in front of them as she spoke.

"The key to the practical application of time-warp was in learning how to create a stable warp field around a starship." A ribbon of light formed in a sinusoidal wave pattern with upward and downward loops of equal size. "As the warp field intensifies, the peaks grow taller and taller until they are juxtaposed in a series of tight loops." She ran her finger up and down the wavy course of the ribbon as she continued to speak. "Traveling linearly along the length of the ribbon would be comparable to the distance we have to travel to get from one peak..." Her finger started at a peak on the curve and followed it down to the bottom of the curve, then again all of the way back up to the next peak of the wave, ending up right next to where she had started. "…to the next. However, by jumping directly from peak to peak…" Her finger jumped back the few centimeters to the peak on which she had started. "…the distance traveled between the points is cut to only a fraction of the linear distance. In short, we go from point A to point B in a fraction of the travel time that would be required without warping space."

She turned to face Danny again. "As I was saying, the theory is quite simple, yet as you know, the applications were so complicated that it was not feasible until the development of New Physics back in the twenty-second century by Dr. Randolf Newton. In the beginning it took a ship full of equipment and a team of physicists to apply the warp theory to space travel, to do what any pilot can now do with a shipboard computer and the push of a few buttons. The time-warp system is equally simplistic in theory," she continued as the holographic images in front of them continued to display her theories in a colorful, three-dimensional array of opalescent light. "However, in the time-warp theory, the two points are at the same location in space, but at different points in time. In short, time has always been thought of as being fixed in a linear pattern, just the way that people used to think about space before the advent of space-warp systems. But just as space was found to have malleable qualities, we've discovered that timelines can also be bent. In short, we've figured out how to warp time."

The holographic images continued to unfold in front of them, depicting each phase of the theory that she was describing. This technique had revolutionized the instruction of spatial relationships, particularly for those individuals not gifted with a keen sense of spatial perception.

"You see," she continued, "any two points in time are connected by a timeline—a line that travels straight through time, rather than space." She touched a point on the ribbon. "Let's say this is 2550…" As she touched the spot, it lit up brightly with a laser point of red light. "…and this is 1800." The second point brightened with a blue light of the same intensity as she touched it. "As the line is 'folded'…" Again a ribbon of light began to bend into an undulating waveform. "…the two points come closer and closer together until the line is nearly folded upon itself, then…"

The ribbon on the trimensional image folded tightly upon itself, and as the points of red and blue approached each other, there was an intense flash of red light streaking from the first point to the second. In a split second, the flash subsided and the second blue point had turned red, the only point now on the ribbon.

"A time jump," whispered Danny. "Of course. Move the points in time together until they are juxtaposed in time just as a space-warp field juxtaposes two points in space. Then we simply jump from one to the other, as we would jump from one point in space to another. We travel the short distance in time in a matter of seconds that it would have taken centuries to travel if we had followed a linear path through time."

"Milliseconds," she corrected him.

"Huh?"

"Milliseconds. The time-warp field we've created can bring together any two predetermined points in time within an eight-hundred-year period within milliseconds of each other. Any time travel longer than that would require a separate jump."

"Then why do I need a copilot to run this thing?"

"Because like the early space-warp systems, this new time-warp system is still in its early stages of development. The controls are bulky and quite complicated. If not handled precisely, your ship would be lost in time. You don't have the time to learn it now, Danny. Captain Beck is the only chance you have of completing your travel successfully."

Stryker turned warily toward Captain Beck and said, "Well then, Beck, I'm glad to have someone of your caliber at the controls," with just a hint of sarcasm in his voice.

Beck stared back evenly. "Likewise, Stryker, we should make one hell of a team."

CHAPTER VI

The Six-shooter

It was a crisp day, and the afternoon gusts stung Danny's cheeks as he turned the corner outside the main entry at Omnicenter Central. There weren't many trees around to signal the change of seasons with their vibrant blush of Fall foliage, and the chill in the air caught Danny by surprise.

The morning briefing had been stressful enough to remind him of why he had not wanted to pursue a military career in the first place, and the strange twist of fate that brought him face to face with Jennifer that morning added to the confusion. A plethora of emotions that he'd forgotten could exist rushed into his soul at the worst possible time, a time in which he had to maintain the utmost indifference to his emotions to focus on the crucial business at hand. But for the first time in many years, Danny had little control of his feelings. He was not in control, and it was unnerving as hell.

As soon as the briefing had ended, he knew he needed to distance himself from Omnicenter Central to regain his composure, and he headed toward the one piece of humanity and serenity that still existed in the area. There was a small park about a mile from the government offices that had been preserved by Dr. Frederick Rinfeld, the founder of Omnicenter. He had battled a great deal of resistance when plans for the technocenter were being developed, but had held his ground. It was well known to all Space Corps Academy graduates who treasured this spot that, at the final planning meeting before his death, Dr. Rinfeld had said simply, "We must never forget where we came from, why we do the things we do, and what we do them for. This park of nature shall stand as a token of our life-blood in a city of unnatural creations." And so it was that in the midst of a mass of steel and concrete conceived and planned by a man of great vision, a man who never lived to see its fruition, there stood a small park of the most beautiful trees and gardens remaining on the continent.

Danny walked briskly in the stimulatingly cool air and shielded his cheeks with his left hand. But as he turned off Rinfeld Boulevard into Park Square Road, his hands dropped to his side. He stared in awe at the beautiful deciduous trees adorned in brilliant shades of red, orange, and gold. He had forgotten the spectacle of Fall.

As he stood staring at nature's last wonder in the sector, he felt a firm but gentle grasp on his left arm. It brought back a rush of memories and he turned knowingly to face the most beautiful woman he had ever seen.

"I've missed you, Danny."

"Me too, Jenni-Lee. More than you could know."

They turned and strolled arm in arm into the park that flowed with memories of the happiest moments of both of their lives. They walked up the mulched path lined with yellow chrysanthemums, and up along the dormant patch of azaleas, which would burst into full pink and red blossoms each Spring. They knew these gardens well, for they remained the same year after year, each replanting following the detailed plans of Dr. Frederick Rinfeld. They walked toward the center of the park and into a small thicket of spruce trees, which still concealed their favorite stone and wrought iron bench, reminiscent of times long gone by. They sat down side-by-side, so familiar in memory, yet so awkward from the years of absence. Slowly and gently, they embraced. And as the grasp of each grew tighter around the other, tears began to flow from the eyes of two people who had been stolid pillars of emotional ambivalence for years.

They held each other more from fear of letting go than out of the tenderness that binds two intimate lovers familiar with the nuances of each other's sinuous grasp. But soon Jennifer's hands began to move slowly and gently up the nape of Danny's neck and comb gently through his thick, brown hair. Every muscle in Danny's body softened and his skin began to tingle. Without realizing it, his hands had slipped to the sides of Jennifer's slim waist as he firmly pulled her body closer to his and turned his face toward hers. He had never forgotten how truly beautiful she was, but he had forgotten how it made him feel to gaze into her dark brown eyes. The tears on their cheeks carried the chill of the air toward their lips as they were drawn toward each other. The warmth that flowed between them as they kissed gave Danny a comfort that he had not known in years.

They held each other closely, taking frequent respites to stare into each other's eyes, but said little as the afternoon slipped away. They were not ready for reminiscing, and neither wanted to broach the experiences of their years of separation for fear of spoiling the precious little time they had together before Danny would have to leave again.

"Danny, I have something for you," she said as they began strolling back toward the perimeter of the park.

"I was hoping you'd ask," Danny said with a wry smile.

Jennifer blushed. "I was hoping *you* would, but that's not what I meant. I have something at the lab, something that I need to give you before you leave tomorrow."

Danny was a bit embarrassed, but his curiosity was piqued.

As they approached Omnicenter, they each assumed an air of formality that disguised the pleasant delirium they each felt from their newly rekindled passion. The two Space Corps officers strode down the corridors with an air of dignity and purpose. As they entered Dr. Lee's office, Danny closed the door behind him and in one motion turned and embraced Jennifer in a passionate kiss not dampened by the cold, wet tears they had wiped from their faces as they left the park together.

Jennifer's back arched rigidly in surprise, then went helplessly limp as she succumbed to her emotions. After an endless moment, she recomposed herself and pulled away half-heartedly.

"Business first, Danny. This is something that may just save your life in the nineteenth century, and I couldn't live with myself if you didn't come back to me because I didn't have time to give it to you."

Jennifer walked over to the far side of the room and touched a fingerprint recognition pad centered just above one of the large ice-blue panels that extended about a meter up from the floor along the length of the wall. The panel immediately below the touch pad lifted out a few centimeters and slid to the left, overlapping the adjacent panel. In the space just vacated by the displaced panel was a series of drawers and cabinets with no visible means of opening them. It was obvious to Danny that this was a voice-activated lock system, one reserved for secure storage, as evidenced by the cost and inconvenience of limiting access to only programmed users.

"Security lock access. Lee, Jennifer. Voice recognition access," droned Jennifer, who, like most scientists inundated with technology, was tired of talking to computers. The second drawer from the top opened slowly, driven methodically out by the servomotor tied into the voice recognition control module. Jennifer reached in quickly but carefully and removed an object. Danny's eyes widened with boyish awe as she handed him a pistol.

"A six-shooter!" he exclaimed in disbelief. "Where did you get this thing? How could you have known that the obelisk would be in 1849 in California?" He couldn't take his eyes off of it. "Is there someplace I can try this thing out?" He was so excited he couldn't wait for the answers, as he grabbed the Colt and twirled it on his finger just the way he'd done a hundred times before in his imagination. "Do you have a holster for this thing? I've got to have a holster. And it's got to be real leather. Does real leather still exist on Earth?"

"Slow down, Danny! And be careful with that thing. It's not what you think."

Danny looked over at her inquisitively. "I know my six-shooters, and this is a Colt for sure."

"I know," she replied. "I designed it after the one in that old picture we had taken at the beach. You know, the one where we dressed up in those old costumes and were superimposed on a digital image of an Old West saloon. Since the picture was digitized, it was a breeze to download the dimensions of that six-shooter you were holding on to. Even though it was just a plastimer toy, its dimensions were authentic enough to fool even you at first. I figured that was good enough for me to work from.

"You see, Danny, I never could get you out of my system. The fact that this is here really has nothing to do with the obelisk or that old picture you brought in, but it has everything to do with you. In fact, you were a big part of my drive to develop the time-warp system in the first place. It was your obsession with the Old West that got me fascinated with the whole concept of time travel. At first it was just my link to you that sparked my interest to join the project, but the project soon became *my* obsession.

"This pistol is my link to you," she said, pointing to the six-shooter. "I've held tight to a fantasy of being able to send you back to a place and time that would fulfill your fantasy, and of the pleasure it would give me to be there to see you enjoy it. But I also remembered all of your stories and pictures, and the Western videos where everybody was always getting shot at. I needed a way to protect you from the past, and to protect the past from you."

Danny knew exactly what she meant. He'd been over and over the age-old scientific dilemma of time travel that had stimulated discussions among sci-fi buffs for the last millennium. If he were to travel back in time to live out his fantasy, he could disturb nothing and change the life of no one without risking changing the course of history and, with that, his own very existence.

Jennifer gingerly removed the pistol from his hands. "This is a bit different from the Colt revolvers in the movies. There are a few things you'd better know about this before you go slinging it around."

She placed the revolver carefully on the table and went back across the room to the open drawer. She reached in and triggered a hidden release switch, opening the cabinet just below the security drawer, a cabinet that had also been concealed by the panel that was now neatly superimposed over the one to the left of it. She bent to reach into the cabinet. As her blue body suit stretched tightly over her shapely form, Danny couldn't help but feel distracted despite his excitement over the six-shooter and his impending journey into the reality of his imagination. She turned back toward him, holding a leather holster and gun belt filled with bullets, undoubtedly the right caliber for the Colt sitting next to him on the table. He couldn't wait to fill the chamber and take aim as he'd done a thousand times in his dreams. He knew he'd be a perfect shot. As she drew closer, his eyes were drawn to one bullet in particular.

"This is the key to what I've been working on for you, Danny," she said, tapping her index finger against the bright silver bullet in the middle of the gun belt. "This bullet contains the circuit implant for a high-powered sonic beam."

Sonic weaponry had been developed in the twenty-first century. It was really a very simple theory using silent but highly-focused, intense sound waves above the audible spectrum to stun a victim senseless. It was easy to fabricate a sonic handgun once compact nucleic cells were developed, providing the high-energy miniature power cells needed to make the weapon portable, and thereby functional. It had been the weapon of choice for most police departments on Earth for several years, until sonic shields became common attire for the criminally inclined.

"Very clever," Danny cut in. "No one in 1849 will know what hit them when they're stopped with a sonic weapon, and no one will get hurt."

He thought for a moment. "But they will be a bit suspicious when I pull my gun and shoot, and they see someone crumple to the ground without hearing a sound."

Jennifer reached for the pistol and inserted the silver bullet into the first chamber. A loud shot rang out as she squeezed the trigger, being careful to aim at the padded target on the wall.

"Whoa!" said Danny, startled as he jumped away and reflexively lifted his hands to his ears.

"I've thought of that," she said simply.

Danny's ears were still ringing from the deafening shot that he'd never imagined would be so loud, as Jennifer began to explain her creation.

"The nucleic cell is sealed into the handle."

"Nucleic!" Danny yelped. "You used nucleic cells?"

Jennifer shook her head in the affirmative. The radioactive waste from spent nucleic cells had been deemed an environmental hazard back in the twenty-fourth century and the Federation had banned the use of all nuclear energy other than that produced by nutonium reactors. Nutonium, found in abundance on Teconea, was an ideal nuclear fuel; it left only inert byproducts, no radioactive waste. It was perfect for large power generators, but did not produce the radioactive material needed for the miniature nucleic cells. It was therefore useless for portable devices. Alternatives, such as antimatter cells, were very expensive, and the Teconean Empire continued to use traditional fuel sources such as uranium-based nucleic cells for their weapons.

"Since when did you turn renegade? You were always the kind of girl who wouldn't even bend a rule, much less break one."

Jennifer smiled coyly. It was nice to know that she wasn't entirely predictable. "I figured this was a good reason to bend a few rules. I couldn't very well stick an antimatter cell into this thing," she said, tapping the gun. "If it got lost back in the nineteenth century, someone might discover how to harness antimatter before mankind is ready for it. It would risk mucking up the timeline too much. Nucleic cells were the only solution. They'll most likely degrade before anyone finds them and, if not, by the time someone figures out what they are, they'll probably be in the nuclear age anyway. Just the same, I'd suggest you don't leave it there to find out."

"So you stole some enriched uranium? I'm impressed," Danny nodded.

"Nothing quite so dramatic…or obtuse," she said with a subtle lift of her left eyebrow.

Danny cringed ever so slightly.

"I scavenged our stash of old Teconean weapons."

"Of course," Danny said. "The Neanderthals never did ban those dirty cells, did they?"

"Nope," Jennifer said, "but it's still illegal to buy Teconean weapons or nucleic cells here. So I rummaged through old weapons that we had confiscated for research. The power cells were all dead, so no one ever bothered taking the weapons apart to dispose of the nuclear waste."

"And dead power cells were useful…how?"

"Most of them still had minute amounts of active material left. Individually, the cells were useless, but over the years, I was able to gather enough radioactive material to make two small cells, and…voila!" she said, holding the gun up as if to shoot.

"No!" Danny yelled, raising his hands up to his ears in a panic.

Jennifer laughed. "Don't worry. I wouldn't want to waste the cells."

"Cute," Danny said, relaxing.

"Anyhow," Jennifer continued, "like I said, I sealed the nucleic cell into the handle. That way, it'll last longer and it's less likely to be discovered in case someone stumbles onto the six-shooter. Besides, I figured you wouldn't have to worry about easy replacement access or recharge ports, since nucleic cells aren't going to be real plentiful in California in 1849. The highly conductive contacts in the shell of the silver bullet will connect with the nucleic cell when the bullet is loaded into the first chamber in the barrel. None of the other chambers will work, except as ports for standard bullets. It will fire chambers two through five just like a normal Colt would, in case you need to do some real shooting to avert suspicion. And since you won't be able to afford to miss what you're aiming at, I've equipped it with a nanocircuit guidance enhancement system tied into the sighting device. Whatever's lined up with the gunsight when you pull the trigger will be hit within one millimeter from the center of sight alignment at a distance of up to one hundred meters."

"I'll be the best sharpshooter in the West!"

"That's hardly the point, cowboy," she continued. "Remember, the idea is to be as *in*conspicuous as possible. Save your lead bullets for target practice. When you need to defend yourself, make sure the silver bullet is loaded. When you fire with the silver bullet in the active first chamber, a sonic pulse will be generated in the direction that the gun is aimed, and, simultaneously, a firing sound will be produced by a sound generator embedded in the handle."

"Yeah," Danny muttered, raising his hand back up over his ear in a futile attempt to muffle the already passed sound waves of the artificial gunshot. "I loved your demonstration."

"This was designed primarily as a 'non-interference' defensive weapon to preserve history and avert suspicion in the nineteenth century, but in an emergency, it has been programmed for a wide field sonic burst of sixty degrees, which can be activated by squeezing the trigger twice in rapid succession."

"A real crowd pleaser," he quipped.

"And a real attention getter. They may be a little curious when you take out twenty men with one shot. Don't use it without a clear escape path. It's unlikely that they would ever figure out how this works even if they get suspicious, but if they're smart enough to preserve it, it could lead to some premature discoveries of nucleics and nanocircuitry in the early twenty-first century."

"I also don't want you coming back full of holes," she continued, "and knowing you, you'll draw plenty of attention. So I added one other little safety feature that should be as foreign to your competition as a sonic blaster. Don't ever take that off," she said pointing to the gun belt, which he had already pulled around his waist. "It's impregnated with a metallic deflection field generator which should adequately deflect any bullets coming at you. The power source is a standard nucleic cell, which is imbedded to avoid accidental detection. This one is in the belt buckle and should give you three months of continuous operation once activated. Activation is automatic when the belt is buckled, so if I were you, I'd take it off now and save the power for another century."

Danny took the six-shooter and placed it in the holster. He then reluctantly took it off and placed it in the padded satchel that Jennifer handed him. "I don't know what to say, Jenni-Lee," he stumbled, stopping to realize for the first time what all this really meant. He was so caught up in the excitement that he hadn't thought about the many hours of work Jennifer had put into this project over the nights and weekends of the past decade. Hours spent just in the hope of one day having the chance to give the six-shooter to him; hours spent just as a way of spending time with the man she painfully missed.

He walked her home, and had forgotten all about the satchel by the doorway long before the morning sun pierced harshly through the window and pried his eyes open from the most peaceful sleep he'd ever had.

CHAPTER VII

Back to the Good-Ole Days

T.C. was already on board the Stargazer, admiring the time-warp drive system that Beck was busy checking over, when Danny walked in. As they looked up, T.C. couldn't help but notice a peaceful look of satisfaction that he'd never seen on Danny's face before, and he didn't need to ask where Danny had been for the past day. Beck was oblivious to it, as he stood up and brushed the wrinkles from his newly-pressed uniform.

"You're late," he said in his usual punctilious manner. "You're the captain of this mission, Stryker, but when I'm on a board we go by the book or we don't go. I have always respected your abilities, but I abhor your style. I hope we have an understanding."

Danny had to bite his lower lip to hold back his laughter. "Absolutely, Captain." He feigned a cough as he turned, barely able to contain himself as he looked at the meticulous Captain Beck standing next to T.C. in his jeans, sneakers and T-shirt, which undoubtedly were cleaner than the tattered leather jacket Danny had slung over his shoulder.

"You O.K., Ace?" T.C. asked with a bit of a smile, as he walked over and put one of his massive arms around Danny's shoulders, accentuating the finely-tuned triceps muscles that resulted from his arduous daily workouts. He practically pulled Danny out the door, which automatically closed behind them as they burst out laughing and slowly fell to the floor. They sat up against a wall and tried to compose themselves as Beck, oblivious as usual to the thoughts of those around him, went on with his final flight prep just on the other side of the door.

"It's going to be a long trip," said Danny, trying hard to regain his composure.

"Yeah, about six hundred and fifty years!" T.C. burst out, as they both lost all control again. They were both in that state of borderline self-control, when even the meekest attempt at comedy could set a man off in uncontrollable laughter, but later leave him wondering what had been funny enough to reduce him to childlike fits for several delirious moments.

They avoided each other's gazes, slowly returning to adulthood.

"Seriously, Danny," T.C. began, with enough sincerity in his voice to avoid a repeat of the giggling that they now felt embarrassed about as they looked around. "We need Beck to get where we're going. Or should I say *when* we're going. You know him as well as I do, maybe better. We're going to have to play it his way to do this thing. He's so inflexible that he could never do the job right if it's not done by the book. He's liable to decompensate if we don't do it his way, and I for one don't want to be stuck somewhere back in time. And remember," he continued recalling Danny's love affair with nineteenth-century California, "you've got something that'll be waiting for you back here in the twenty-fifth century that I don't think you'll want to leave behind again." Danny just smiled as the two men got up and reentered the engine room of the Stargazer.

"Glad to see you two decided to grace me with your presence again," quipped Beck. "We're set to go."

Danny and T.C. glanced at each other inquisitively.

"Just like that!" Danny said, stunned at how quickly the modifications had been completed.

"Just like that," returned Beck. "There's really not much to the installation or operation. Jenny did such a good job with the R&D on this thing that it looks as simple as a kid's music chip player from the outside, which is the only part you guys need to know about. Whatever you do, though, don't muck around with the interior relays of the unit, or you might mess it up so bad that even I can't fix it in 1849, and I sure don't want to live out my days in that primitive dust bowl of an existence."

"You just make sure that thing does its job, and let us do ours," Danny snorted, as he brusquely maneuvered his way past Beck to drop his bag off in his small quarters before preparing to launch. He closed the door of his room behind him. It was an eight foot square cubicle, hardly luxurious for a captain's quarters, but typical for a Class D mission starship. It was ample for his needs. Jennifer had already programmed in his access codes and the room was as secure as she could make it. He could live with that.

He took the short walk to his cot and reached for two small, barely-discernible fingerprint I.D. latches under its front edge. Jennifer had equipped this room with something no one in the twenty-fifth century would expect—a manually accessed secret compartment. Of course, the added security of fingerprint I.D. latches didn't hurt.

He reached down, carefully placing his two index fingers over the latches under the edge of the bunk and heard a faint click. He lifted the front of the bunk, which was hinged at the back, turning it into a lid for a small underlying secret compartment that was created in the dead space behind the four drawers that pulled out from under the bed, standard storage space in most ships' quarters. Using his access code, he opened the small, computer-controlled panel of the hidden compartment and slipped in the satchel containing his six-shooter.

The three men took their positions on the small bridge of the Stargazer, and waited for clearance from air traffic control at the Omnicenter Spaceport. T.C. and Stryker were at the helm plotting a standard take-off and orbit pattern into the navigational control, and Beck was a few meters behind them at the engineering station. There was an eerie silence as even Danny Stryker became serious at the prospect of what lay ahead.

Clearance came quickly and the Stargazer silently lifted in a straight vertical ascent. Within seconds it was in a standard orbital pattern that took them over the vast azure of the Atlantic Ocean headed toward the east coast of the North American Continent, and then toward the Pacific. As they crossed the landmass of North America, the navigational computer confirmed that they had attained a stable orbital pattern. As soon as they were centered over the Pacific where amateur spacecraft tracking—a popular hobby for high school nerds these days—was at a minimum, Beck engaged the time-warp drive.

When the three men regained consciousness, they were somewhat disoriented.

"Check the time clock," Danny muttered to T.C..

"Ten forty-three point four five. We were only out for a few seconds."

"That's to be expected," said Beck dryly. "But look at your log date readout, and then recalibrate based on star position."

"Incredible!" gasped T.C. as the recalculated date appeared. "03.02.1849—six hundred and fifty years in the blink of an eye."

"I've got to hand it to you and Jennie on this one, Beck. The accuracy is astounding. Based on what they were all wearing in that old picture, it had to be summertime when it was taken. We should be within a couple of months of when it was shot."

"Plot a landing course for the canyon area of the desert, Stryker. We should be able to hide the ship in one of the ridges."

"Right. We'll be down in a minute. Secure for landing."

Danny activated the antigravity thrusters as he skillfully guided the ship down toward Palm Canyon in the darkness of the early morning desert. He wanted to get the ship down and well-concealed before daylight. Through the porthole windows nothing could be seen of the rugged landscape, hidden by the blackness of nightfall in the desert during a new moon. The landing time had been carefully chosen. Thanks to the stereotactic radar imagers that the Stargazer, and most modern ships capable of terralandings, were equipped with, the holoscreen displayed the high-resolution, three-dimensional image of the desert landscape as clearly as if the midday sun had been lighting the way.

Danny located a small landing in an opening in the palm-lined canyon, well off the main crevice. A narrow stream trickled quietly through the stately thousand-year-old palms for which this canyon was named, dwarfing the sparse underbrush. The ship fit neatly into the landing and was easily concealed by the rocks and helped with a few strategically-placed palm fronds. The three men sat and waited for the break of daylight to begin their mission. Danny was trembling with excitement. He couldn't believe that he was actually here.

The morning sunlight peered over the mountaintop that marked the border of the canyon and reflected off of the large green fronds that stood starkly out from the vast grayness of the surrounding desert. The men from Omnicenter had never seen so much open, uninhabited land, and even Beck cracked a longing smile as he gasped in awe at the break of day. Within a few minutes, the sunlight poured down into the canyon, illuminating the beauty of this rare stream in the middle of the desert.

Dressed in the appropriate garb, Danny and T.C. headed out of the landing that concealed the ship and walked toward the end of the canyon. Hans Beck stayed behind to safeguard the Stargazer from unsuspecting wanderers. It was about a five-mile walk to the small town of Destin, where Danny would try to trade some recently-replicated currency for a couple of horses. He hoped that the money they had reproduced from the museum was authentic. He knew enough about the Old West to know what they did to counterfeiters and horse thieves.

A slight chill remained in the morning air as they made their way down into the main crevice of the canyon. They walked briskly along the riverbed, unaccustomed to the cool, dry air of the desert morning. As they approached the foothills of the small mountain range that bordered the canyon, the full light of day was upon them. They squinted against the discomfort of the harsh sunlight, annoyingly aware of the fact that their solar visors would be a bit out of place with their otherwise-comfortable costumes of denim and flannel.

"These boots are going to take some getting used to, Ace, but the rest of this get-up is a lot better than synthetics. You actually feel a little fresh air through this stuff. I just wish I had a good pair of moldform shoes for this walk."

"Yeah, my feet are already mapping out my new blisters for me. Whew!" Danny, sighed, taking off his hat to fan himself. "The sun sure comes up quick around here."

They were only about a mile into their walk when they became acutely aware of what the desert was famous for.

"Don't drink too much of that water now, buddy. You're going to need it a lot more at high noon," Danny said with a wry smile, enjoying the chance to use some cowboy lingo.

"Cute. Real cute," T.C. smirked, as he put his canteen back in his pack.

The walk was arduous for two men who were used to the comforts of the twenty-fifth century, but the early-morning start allowed them to arrive in town before the heat of day. Destin was a small town that had developed as a stopping point for miners making their way from Mexico up toward the promised land of gold in Northern California. Not many stayed behind in this parched piece of land on the desert's edge, but those who did were good hard-working people who had decided to avoid the throngs of unsuccessful would-be millionaires and opt for building a life on the business those more adventurous than themselves would bring here during their infrequent stops. There was little excitement here, but it was a peaceful life, with no one fighting to take the nearly worthless land away from them. No one raised an eyebrow when Danny and T.C. strolled into town. Destinites were used to seeing all kinds of people here from all kinds of places. Strangers meant welcome business.

The livery stable was near the edge of town, but the nouveau cowboys couldn't resist the temptation of the "Saloon" sign prominently displayed in the center of the small Main Street. They were both too parched to say anything. They shot a quick glance at each other and headed for the saloon side by side. Danny marveled as he swung open the bifold louvered saloon doors, just as he'd done a thousand times in his dreams. The two men strode uncomfortably up to the bar in their still-too-new boots and sat on stools across from the barkeep, who was setting up for the day.

"Early start, eh boys?" he said, as he smiled at the two men squirming awkwardly on the stools.

"You don't know the half of it," whispered T.C., his speech hushed by the dryness that the desert air had left in his throat. "Give me a nice cold willowberry juice with crushed ice, would ya?"

The barkeep's face tilted to the side inquisitively. "I'm sorry stranger. I don't believe I heard you. Doc says my ears are going."

"Two beers would be fine," Danny said sharply, giving T.C. a gentle kick on the shin. "My friend here has a strange sense of humor."

The barkeep just shrugged his shoulders and scratched the sparse crop of white hair on his head as he turned toward the tap.

"*Un poco loco, eh, hombre?*" grinned a short, dark man at the end of the bar looking toward Danny. "The summer sun here can do that to a man, no?" he said, chuckling as he threw a coin on the counter and grabbed his hat, heading out the door. "I guess it's time to get to work now, Harry," he said to the barkeep. "Adios until the siesta, amigo."

"My best customer," Harry laughed, as he put the mugs down in front of the two men.

They grabbed their mugs, lifted them high and tapped them together as the foam ran down the sides of the thick glass mugs. "I love this place," Danny said as he lifted the drink to his parched lips. They both took a good long guzzle, set their beers down and smiled.

"Too bad we got work to do, Danny."

"Yeah," Danny said longingly. "Too bad."

They finished their drinks quickly, and then cajoled some water out of the bartender after deciding that beer might not be the best way to get hydrated if they were to have any chance of actually staying on the horses they were about to buy. "Much obliged," Danny said with a satisfied smile as they left the bar. Their money seemed to be genuine enough to do the trick.

As much as he wanted to stay and soak up the flavor of this classic frontier town, Danny knew that time might well be of the essence. They really had no way of knowing exactly when that old Billy Delaney Wild West Show picture was taken, or exactly where, for that matter. It was imperative that they locate Billy Delaney *before* the picture was taken. That was the only way to be sure that he would lead them to the obelisk.

The sun bore down on the two men as they made their way down the dusty Main Street to the livery stable. Danny wasn't much of a negotiator, and certainly didn't know the going price of horses in 1849. The local rancher who happened upon them in the livery stable that day was, like most folks in Destin, an honest man, but made a tidy enough profit to go home with quite a smile that day. Danny figured he hadn't exactly made the deal of the century, but mounted his horse with a quiet look of satisfaction. Holosuite riding was surprisingly close to the real thing, he now decided. But somehow the computer-created holosuite lacked the character and feel of a real horse, and certainly lacked the aroma.

"Damn, this thing is bumpy!" T.C. said, as his huge frame bounced awkwardly from side to side.

Danny was a bit more graceful due to his years of practice in the holosuite, but after a few lessons, the athletic T.C. McGee did surprisingly well. The two men headed toward the foothills of the mountain range that concealed Palm Canyon. From his old books, Stryker knew that Billy Delaney's Wild West Show had operated out of a town called Arrowhead, California. The horse trader who so gladly sold them their steeds was only too happy to give T.C. and Danny directions to the local town of Arrowhead, now being frequented by many of Destin's visitors thanks to the growing fame of the Wild West Show. They followed the directions along a canyon pathway. The mountainous walls of the trail were considerably shorter than those which lined Palm Canyon. There was no stream and no growth here other than occasional sagebrush. It was indeed desolate, and an eerie silence surrounded the two men each time they stopped for a brief sip from their priceless canteens. After about an hour's ride, which seemed like an eternity to the unaccustomed horsemen, they stopped for their third break.

"Is that thunder? I don't see a cloud in the sky."

The rumbling was getting gradually louder.

"An earthquake!" yelled T.C., his horse rearing back as he suddenly shifted his massive body backward.

"Do you feel anything, turkey?" asked Danny. "I'm impressed with your knowledge of twentieth-century seismology, but living through an earthquake is a little different than seeing it on an old 2-D flat screen movie. You usually feel something. You know, like the ground trembling, mountains falling, the earth under your feet splitting open—that kind of stuff."

"I get the picture," said T.C. feeling a bit silly.

"What're those dust clouds out there?"

"Horses, and there coming real fast."

"You don't suppose they realized our money was fake, do you?"

"Even if they did, these guys are coming from the east. Their communication systems aren't good enough in nineteenth century California for them to have already called the cops in another town, and we've been heading due east of Destin for an hour now."

The riders quickly approached as the two men talked.

"Well, at the very least, I think we ought to get out of the way."

"Right," T.C. said, as they turned back to a fork they had just passed in the road.

As they reached the turnoff, the first two riders in the group rode swiftly past them. From their frenetic pace, Danny surmised that they were outlaws, and that the group of riders following close behind was a posse. Danny, who for the first time in his life was fashion-conscious with the garb of the Old West that enamored him so much, couldn't help but notice that the two outlaws were dressed strikingly like T.C. and himself.

"We'd better make ourselves scarce, and fast," Danny said to T.C., turning and heading down the trail opposite that taken by the two apparent outlaws as quickly as he could manage to get his horse to move.

"Hee-yah!" T.C. yelled, cajoling his horse to follow, struggling to keep up with his more experienced partner.

As they glanced back, much to their dismay, the posse was now following them instead of the outlaws.

"This real enough for you, cowboy?" shrieked T.C. as they kicked their steeds into high gear.

"Follow me," Danny shouted as he passed T.C. riding around a bend in the canyon road. He made a sharp right turn into a small side crevice of the canyon just as a wind whipped through the canyon floor in the opposite direction. They came to an abrupt stop about a hundred yards up the small crevice that dead-ended in a small bluff. The pounding of the hooves of a dozen horses was thundering up the canyon, getting louder and louder.

"I wonder what crime those fellows committed that we're going to get hanged for," T.C. whispered.

The fear on their faces gradually eased as the stampeding noise began to fade in the other direction. "They must have stayed on the main path and followed the dust trail from that wind gust. Thank goodness they don't have any scanners."

"We'd better get out of here before they realize they're chasing a dust storm."

The two men headed out of the crevice and doubled back toward Arrowhead. As they trotted around the bend out of the hidden little trail that had saved their lives, neither of them noticed the faint reflection coming off the dust-coated six-shooter that had fallen out of Stryker's gun belt as he had darted for safety in a state of panic.

CHAPTER VIII

Billy D

Arrowhead, California, was a private ranch owned by one Hickory T. Johnson from a land purchase deal in 1836. Johnson was a very successful Texas cattle rancher who had made his fortune with razor sharp business acumen and a generous helping of luck. By the ripe old age of forty-three, he had become bored with the cattle industry and had amassed more money than he knew what to do with. In the spring of 1835, he shocked the Texas plains communities by selling off his herds of prized cattle, and donating his ranch land to the church. He transferred his savings to the Bank of California, and headed west to pursue his dream of taming a piece of the new wilderness. His path took him to the young, one-horse town of Destin, California, where he instantly fell in love with the harsh yet peaceful existence of this desert border town. He fell even more deeply in love with the sheriff's daughter, Belle.

Belle Landry was Sheriff Landry's pride and joy. She inherited his free spirit and aptitude for sharpshooting, much to her mother's dismay. By the time she was fourteen, she was the star attraction at the town fair, shooting the center out of a gold piece tossed behind her while she rode backwards on a bareback horse. She honed her skills through the years, and taught them to those of the town youth whose parents would tolerate it. A young man three years her junior moved to Destin with his parents in 1830 and quickly became her biggest fan. Billy was the only child of Henry Delaney, who had moved from Boston with his wife, Bess, to help run the general store his brother had started a few years earlier.

Billy was a bright boy, but was a bit small for his age and couldn't always see well through the scratched-up lenses of his eyeglasses. He was, however, a fanatic about gunslingers and western lore, and was ecstatic when his parents decided to join Uncle Bob in Destin. Shortly after their arrival, Billy saw Belle Landry perform at the eleventh annual Destin town fair. He immediately became her biggest fan and most dedicated pupil. Unfortunately, his grace and coordination lagged far behind his fortitude and imagination. But he never gave up.

By 1836, when Hickory T. Johnson rode into town, Belle was an athletic, stunning-looking woman of twenty-three. Although she was the prettiest girl in the territory, she was too intimidating for the young men of Destin and too mistrusting of the wayward fortune hunters who were making their way through town in increasing numbers as rumors spread of the plentiful gold being unearthed in the California Territory. Hickory T. Johnson was different. He was a self-assured man who had never met a human being who could intimidate him. He was invigorated by the strength that he saw in Belle and, like most men, was immediately taken by her beauty. However, unlike most men, in fact unlike any man before him, he quickly swept Belle off her feet. They were married in the spring of 1836, six weeks after Hickory Johnson rode into town.

Hickory Johnson was a man of action, and as soon as he saw Belle ride and shoot he foresaw the fruits of his dream, a dream that Belle would soon come to share, and one that cemented the bond that led to their marriage. Hickory loved this land as much as his new bride, but couldn't stand to reside for too long in any city, not even one as small as Destin. As soon as young Belle said "I do," he sealed a deal to purchase a two-thousand-acre parcel that sat about two hours west of Destin as the horse trots, nestled in the foothills of the mountains. He and Belle moved there in the spring of 1836, and developed a ranch to house and train performers for their new Wild West Show.

Billy Delaney, much to his parents' chagrin, was their first pupil and ranch-hand. Although embarrassingly short on talent, he had become one of Belle's best friends over the years. He wanted to help with the development of the show any way that he could. Of course, his dream would always be to become the star.

Word quickly spread of the new ranch built on the rim of Arrowhead Canyon, and with Johnson's money hanging out as bait, some of the finest horsemen and sharpshooters in the country began to filter in. Through the 1830's they held two shows a year in Destin, with the main show at the Town Fair each year. By 1841, they were drawing crowds from thousands of miles around. People would come to them wherever they were, so they decided to build a permanent rodeo on the ranch, rather than moving all their equipment to Destin each year. Demand was so great for entertainment in the territory that by 1845, shows were being held monthly. To support the large numbers of travelers, the Johnsons built a hotel and restaurant that his brother Howard came to run. A saloon followed shortly thereafter, as did a bank to support the financial needs of the people, most of whom had purchased small parcels of land from Hickory Johnson so they could live near the show that they worked for.

After the schoolhouse was built in 1846, the people decided it was time to incorporate into a township. Although very self-assured, Hickory Johnson was not a pompous man; he declined when the name Johnsonville was proposed for the town. His suggestion of Arrowhead, after the old Indian name of the canyon next to which the town was built, was quickly ratified. And thus the rapid birth of the now-famous town of Arrowhead, California, was complete.

*   *   *   *   *   *   *   *

Henry and Bess Delaney lived in modest quarters above the general store that provided their livelihood. They had worked hard to make a life for themselves in Destin, and to raise their only son the best they could. They were disappointed in what Billy had done with his life, but mainly blamed themselves for moving him away from the sophistication of Boston where he had excelled in grade school. Despite their disappointment, they were still very proud of their son, and looked forward to the weekends he spent with them. Sunday brunch was the best meal of the week for Billy. He treasured his time with his parents, but by Sunday afternoon the topic of conversation would always turn to Billy's future, so he made a habit of leaving soon after the meal.

A plate of scrambled eggs, bacon and hash browns along with a slice or two of freshly baked bread to wipe up the extra bacon grease was a wonderful way to start a Sunday, but a tough way to start a two-hour ride through the desert on horseback. Billy had made this trip hundreds of times through the years, and probably knew the trail better than anyone. His favorite stopping point was a small side crevice, which led to a quiet shady dead-end clearing. It was about an hour into the trip, just before the trail forked off with the east road heading toward Arrowhead, and the north fork heading toward a junction to the San Francisco trail which was heavily traveled by the northbound prospectors.

After an hour of riding, Billy was glad to see the crevice entrance up ahead. The usual desolate entryway was marked with fresh hoof prints, and Billy proceeded cautiously. It looked like there were two sets of tracks leading in and two more leading out. He was fairly certain that whoever had ventured in this way had discovered quickly that it was a dead end trail and had left the same way they came. He dismounted to take a closer look before entering. He studied the tracks and listened for any sound that should easily be heard rumbling out of the small cul de sac. He satisfied himself that his original supposition was right and that his treasured rest stop was indeed abandoned as usual. Just as he turned to remount his horse, a bright glint of light reflected up toward him from the base of the rocky entranceway.

He walked over and brushed a thin layer of dust off the hidden polished metal barrel of Danny Stryker's Colt revolver. He looked over his shoulder and scanned the area to make sure that the recent visitors to his private oasis were really long gone, then reached over and gingerly lifted the revolver from the ground.

"Damn. This thing don't look as it's ever been fired."

He'd only dreamed of having a new Colt, a luxury he could never come close to affording. He looked around again and carefully tucked the gun into his belt. Taking his horse by the reins, he proceeded cautiously to the shady bluff at the end of the crevice. He settled down in the shade and studied his new prize. He opened the barrel and saw that it had five rounds loaded, then closed and spun the barrel. Slipping away into a fantasy he'd had a thousand times before, he spun the gun nimbly around his right index finger, and in a single motion took aim at the top of a small rock formation on the ridge fifty yards away and squeezed the trigger. The tip of the rock exploded into fragments. Billy's jaw dropped as he stared at his target in disbelief. He'd been taking aim at that rock every week for years and took pride in the chip that his bullet had once made only a foot from its target. He glanced down at the revolver in his hand.

"Well I'll be. It *is* the gun."

Billy was always convinced that with the right gun he could shoot as well as anybody, even Belle. In fact, he'd tried dozens of guns, even a new revolver that Belle once let him borrow. But none of them ever felt quite right, and up until now the results had always been the same.

He pulled out his old revolver and took aim at the newly-shaped target his last bullet had created. He fired and stared in vain for the destination of his shot which sailed so high of the mark that its trail was instantly lost. He picked up the new Colt, twirled and fired again. He smiled as his target again burst into dust.

"Maybe it's my style," he smirked as he reached for his old pistol, twirled it on his finger and shot off another round. Only by the ricochet sound coming from the hillside to his right could he tell that his bullet had actually hit something. This was a bad shot even for him. "I guess not," he muttered.

He again hoisted the new Colt and squeezed off three rounds in rapid succession, each hitting their target before he had lowered the gun to his side.

"I always knew it was just a matter of time."

He was really feeling his oats now. He reloaded the Colt, anxious to fire off six more rounds. The same five chambers that were loaded when he found the gun easily reloaded, but much to his chagrin Billy just couldn't get the sixth round to load into the chamber. He tried cleaning it, but still no luck. He studied the chamber carefully and concluded that it was just drilled the wrong size. Five perfect chambers would have to do.

"Billy Delaney's five-shooter," he snickered. "Sounds good to me."

He took a penny out of his pocket and tossed it high in the air. He drew his pistol and fired quickly.

"Damn, I'm good," he said, as he inspected the penny with a new hole in the dead center.

He took out two more pennies and tossed them into the air. He drew and shot twice from the hip in rapid succession. The pennies were unmarred. He tossed them up again, but aimed more carefully as he squeezed off two shots. This time the six-shooter was pointed close enough to the vicinity of its target for the guidance system to do its job, and he was a bit more satisfied as he inspected his work.

"I am good. Real good. Billy D…. a real class act…finally," he said to himself.

Billy D. headed off toward Arrowhead with a newfound sense of pride and the renewed determination of a nearly abandoned dream. The next show was Sunday, and he couldn't wait to talk to Belle.

    *   *   *   *   *   *   *   *

Stryker and McGee turned off of the main path again shortly after passing the fork in the road. Realizing the posse had picked up the trail of the two *real* bandits, they felt it was safe to continue north toward the San Francisco trail. Just the same, they decided their choice of clothing wasn't the best if they didn't want to be mistaken for bandits again. They quickly changed into the spare shirts they had brought with them and burned their unlucky shirts to avert further problems. They had seen the two bandits ride right past them earlier, and up close they looked different enough from the two men who had robbed Howard Johnson's hotel that morning; they felt sure they would have no further problems.

They rode along the trail toward Arrowhead and trotted into the bustling town by midafternoon. Arrowhead was much different from the quaint solitude of Destin. Its rapid expansion and frequent visitation by the entertainment-starved wealthy lent it the luxurious air of opulence rarely seen except in big cities. Although exhausted from the travails of the day, Danny and T.C. rode up and down Main Street soaking in the ambience. They were dying to quench their thirst in the saloon, but they dreaded the pain of trying to walk after a day of riding. It had been agony getting back up on their horses after their brief rest earlier in the afternoon, and they were sure they'd look like clowns trying to get back on their horses again today if they took another break.

As they headed back to the livery stable to board their horses before checking into the hotel, they didn't notice the jubilant Billy Delaney galloping past them, headed for the Johnsons' Arrowhead ranch.

CHAPTER IX

The Prime Directive

After suffering through an hour sitting at the table for a dinner they were too tired to savor, Danny and T.C. went up to their room. The stairs looked endless; fortunately they were on the first floor above the lobby.

"City slickers," the innkeeper chuckled to himself, watching the two men struggling up the stairs. It was obvious they hadn't done much riding in their time.

The room was nicely done, like everything else in town. As tired as he was, Danny still marveled at the abundance of wood and leather which made up all of the furnishings. As he slipped off his gun belt, a sickening feeling overwhelmed him. T.C. looked up as Stryker exhaled in a puff of disgust.

"What's wrong, cowboy? I thought you loved this stuff," T. C. said as he struggled out of his boots. "Change your mind about the glamour of the Old West?"

T.C. didn't know about the six-shooter Jennifer had made for Danny. He was puzzled by the look on Stryker's ashen face, staring down at the empty holster.

"Lose your play toy, Ace?" he laughed. "You know you can't shoot anybody anyway. It sure makes me nervous being around all these guns without my phaser, even if they are primitive lead slingers. But you know the prime directive, we can't take a chance of shooting anybody anyway."

The prime directive was a catch phrase borrowed from a popular old television show about space travelers. In the show it referred to the prime directive of non-interference in other more primitive cultures to avoid affecting their evolution. In time travel it was even more pertinent, and was well known to every cadet who dreamed of participating in time travel missions that were rumored to be nearly a reality for the Omnicenter scientists. Of course, these rumors had persisted for decades, but every class of cadets was sure that time travel would be perfected for them. It was ironic that Stryker and T.C. McGee, who had long ago given up that dream, would be the first. They were, however, acutely aware of the prime directive and the need to minimize the influence they would have on anybody in the nineteenth century.

"You don't understand, buddy. The focus of our mission has just changed."

Danny explained the inner workings of Dr. Lee's six-shooter to T.C., and the potential threat that it posed to the timeline. Although Jennifer had tried to minimize the risk of losing the gun back in the nineteenth century by using a nucleic cell rather than an antimatter cell, the risk was still a very real concern. Even though it was unlikely that nineteenth-century humans would figure out the technology behind Danny's six-shooter, it was entirely possible that within the next two hundred years, someone could conceivably accelerate the discovery of nuclear energy and change the future of humanity if the gun were to fall into the wrong hands.

The obelisk was a different story; they already knew that it had somehow withstood the test of time. It was a known quantity in history, at least the end result of a history that saw it in the 1849 Wild West Show. But the pistol was an unknown. It had to be recovered before they returned to the twenty-fifth century.

It was already dusk. The search would have to start tomorrow.

CHAPTER X

Double Trouble

Stryker and McGee awakened with the sun on the second floor of the Howard Johnson Hotel in Arrowhead.

"I don't believe I can move," muttered T.C.. "I ain't tired, I just can't move."

Danny just groaned.

"I didn't know I had some of these muscles."

"And you used to think football practice was tough," Danny joked, as he grabbed his side from the pain of his weak laugh. "Damn!"

"Yeah, but I was a kid then. You're not supposed to hurt when you're nineteen. We're old men now. Real old," he groaned as he tried to pry his body out of bed.

"Speak for yourself. I'm not half as old as I feel."

About one hour and two pots of some of the worst coffee they'd ever tasted later, they started to feel human again.

"I don't feel like getting on that horse any more than you do, but we've got to get an early start. Between the gun and the obelisk, we've got double trouble. We need to find that gun real quick."

"*We?*" said T.C. turning his head with the most animation Danny had seen from him all day. "What's this *we* stuff? I believe that *you* are the one who forgot to strap down your sidearm, sir. I'll just wait upstairs till you get back. Just give a little knock when you're ready for me, O.K.?"

"Oh right. Sure. *No* problem!" Danny got up from the table. "Meet me at the livery stable in ten minutes."

T.C. just groaned.

Danny had already finished checking the saddles on their horses when T.C. walked in. He stiffened up at the odor that greeted him as he walked through the open doorway to the stables.

"Man!" he groaned. "This is glamour, huh?"

Danny walked the horses up to greet him. "Great stuff, ain't it?"

They both looked painfully up at their saddles, which they could swear were at least a foot further off the ground today. The stable hand just laughed and shook his head. Used to seeing city folks coming into town for the show, he just pretended that Stryker and McGee blended right in with the local horsemen.

"Looks like a hot one, fellas. Make sure your canteens is all full up," he said as he turned to get back to his work.

They grimaced and painstakingly lifted their left legs into the stir-rups, then heaved their bodies up over the patiently waiting horses that they had purchased the day before. They turned right out of the stable and trotted slowly a quarter of a mile out past the grand arch that welcomed visitors to the posh town of Arrowhead. The turn-off to Destin was a half-mile ahead to the left, and they slowly made their way, vigilant for any sign of the lost Colt revolver. It was going to be a long day.

By the time they had made their way back to the bluff where they had rested the day before, the sun was high overhead and the shade at the end of the bluff was very inviting. They dismounted much more nimbly than they had mounted a few hours before, having loosened up considerably during the leisurely ride.

"Needle in a haystack," Danny said in disgust.

"Big, hot, dusty haystack," T.C. affirmed as he lowered his muscular body to a low rock nestled deep into the shadows of the adjacent bluff. His eyes stopped at a small dusty clearing across the bluff to his right. He smiled as the metallic glint hit his eye. "Hell, you must have wandered over there while I was quivering in my boots yesterday."

"What?" Danny said as he turned from his horse. He saw T.C. starting toward the small clearing. "I don't remember moving from…"

"Damn! They're just shells."

Danny walked up behind him. "Let me see those."

He inspected the five shells that T.C. had just lifted from the dusty ground, and brushed away the dust from the casing of one of them. He stared blankly as his hand dropped to his side clutching the shells.

"Somebody's been here since we left yesterday," said T.C. dryly, noticing the footprints in the dirt. "I remember staring over here from that same rock, and marveling at how deserted everything seemed to be." It was a sharp contrast to the crowded Earth he'd grown up in.

"And that somebody has my revolver," Danny said dryly, holding up the shell he'd just cleaned off. There was a faint rainbow hue to the reflection. These shells are a viridium alloy. They didn't use viridium until the twenty-fourth century.

"We'd better get back to the Stargazer. The on-board scanners are our best bet of finding that pistol before whoever's got it leaves town."

It was mid afternoon by the time the two men reached the Stargazer, having taken the time to dust the trail behind them with a palm frond on their way into the small canyon where the Stargazer was camouflaged. Beck heard the clopping of the horses' hooves landing flatly against the hard, dusty floor of the canyon, and was standing ready with a hand phaser behind a rocky ledge next to the ship as the two men approached. He was getting ready to fire when he recognized his shipmates.

"What are you doing with those filthy animals?" he snarled.

"The local magnetocraft dealer was completely out of stock. Can you believe it?" Danny answered tongue in cheek.

"Cute, Stryker. Real cute. You boys were better than I thought. I figured it would take you a week just to find the obelisk, much less figure out a way to get possession of it."

The two men still on their horses looked at each other sheepishly. They hated to give Beck anything to gloat about, but didn't have much of a choice.

"We don't exactly have it yet," started T.C..

"Not exactly?" asked Beck with a look of disdain coming over his smug face. It was always smug.

Danny smiled as he thought back to that last wonderful day that he and Jennifer had spent together reviewing the mission. "He was probably born with that expression," he had mused to her. It had only been a couple of days ago, but already seemed an eternity to Danny.

"Not *exactly*?" Beck repeated a bit more loudly.

"Well actually, we really don't have a clue where it is yet," answered Danny, as the ethereal image of a scantily-clad Jennifer Lee abruptly evaporated from his mind.

"That is," continued T.C., "we have a clue, just not an exact location. Only we need to find the six-shooter first."

"Six-shooter?" Beck asked as his disdainfully-twisted face shifted to a look of blank confusion. "What's a six-shooter?"

Danny hated having to tell Beck about the gun, much less having to admit to him that he had lost the damn thing.

"Just something I promised Jen I'd pick up for her," he said giving T.C. a sharp slap on the back. He figured that if he could just get to the scanners on board the Stargazer, he might be able to locate the gun and get it back without having to explain himself to his already-distrustful partner. "But that can wait. We need access to the ship's scanners to help pinpoint the location of the obelisk."

Beck looked at him with the characteristically nauseating air of superiority that had always insured him of a lack of friends. "What makes you think the scanners will be of any more use now? We couldn't find a trace of vitanium with our initial scan."

Danny grinned. "But now we have some idea of distance and direction, we can run an enhanced scan on a coned-down area and may be able to confirm the location before we waste any more time in Arrowhead." Danny had almost forgotten how much fun one-upsmanship was when Beck was around.

T.C. had been working with Danny enough years to take the cue.

"Give me a hand, will you?" he said to Beck. "I took a nasty fall the first time I tried to get on this animal and my knee's getting so stiff I can hardly walk."

Beck, who had started toward the ship with Stryker, hesitated and looked at T.C. who grimaced in agony as he reached down toward his right knee. Beck had been a medic during his first tour of duty on the border. He was proud of his medical skills, and T.C. knew it. He was too proud of a chance to show off his skills to not take the bait. This would give Danny the time he needed to adjust the sensors for a viridium scan and locate the six-shooter before Beck knew what was going on.

Beck looked back toward Danny who continued toward the ship, and then apprehensively turned and started over to help his wounded comrade off of the horse that he desperately wanted to avoid.

"How can you stand the smell of live animals?" he snarled, contorting his face to angle his nose away from the steed.

"It's kind of nice once you get used to...Oww!" screeched T.C. as he fell to the ground grabbing his knee.

Danny was grateful to have a partner like T.C.. *That guy should have gone into theater*, he mused to himself.

Danny went to work quickly. He was as well-versed in scanner technology as any pilot in the fleet, and in a few minutes had the gun located somewhere in a five-hundred-square-meter radius that fell within the borders of Arrowhead. He was just finishing readjusting the scanners for a vitanium trace when Beck came up behind him.

"A bit rusty with scanner controls, eh, Stryker?" he smirked, the smugness returning to its natural state.

"Yeah," replied Danny obsequiously. "I guess I need help from the expert on this one." *He's just egotistical enough to believe that,* Danny thought. *This guy's easier to play than a drum.*

Beck was competent with scanner technology, but much less proficient than Stryker. Danny was dying to shove him out of the way and finish the job, but he impatiently allowed Beck to methodically lumber through the scan.

"There's your obelisk," he stated emphatically with a look of superiority.

Danny wanted to break his face.

"Good work, Beck." He could taste the blood as he bit his lip. *This is your own fault,* he thought to himself. *Next time keep the damned gun strapped in.*

The vitanium scan placed the obelisk in almost the exact same perimeter of space as the six-shooter.

"Outstanding," whispered Danny to himself realizing that he could go after the six-shooter without having to arouse any suspicion in Beck.

"Thanks," said Beck. " I pride myself in my scanner tech proficiency."

Danny and T.C. smiled as they headed back out of the ship.

"You ought to give that knee some rest," Beck shouted at T.C. as he headed for his horse.

"It feels like a million," he answered, not sure exactly where that expression had come from, like so many other expressions drawn from a past—and now incomprehensible—reference. "You're a miracle worker."

I only examined him. He wouldn't even let me give him an anti-inflammatory application, Beck thought, shrugging his shoulders as he walked back to the ship to resume his vigil. Stryker and McGee weren't his favorite companions, but he realized that he had actually enjoyed the break from the monotony of guarding an abandoned ship.

Chapter XI

Time Bandits

Danny and T.C. hadn't yet seen the show, and were probably the only men in town who didn't know about the object they'd traveled centuries to find. The obelisk was always prominently displayed in the archway to the arena, where the performers entered. The glint of the sun scattered off of it brilliantly, sending rays in every direction. No one who saw it could ever forget it, including some of the more unsavory citizens of the West. Rumor had it that the obelisk was made of the purest silver and gold ever found. It was only the thought of trying to pull off a burglary in the midst of the finest sharpshooters in the West that kept the riffraff away.

Hickory T. Johnson I, the grandfather of Arrowhead's first citizen, had been a British nobleman with a long history of loyalty to the crown. He had been the up and coming patriarch of the Johnson estate in Yorkshire when the French Revolution broke out in 1789. Like many of the British nobility, his empathy lay with the French noblemen who were being hunted down along with their wives and children to be imprisoned and beheaded for the crime of having been born into wealth. He had joined a secret society of young British aristocrats who had successfully infiltrated Paris with the help of some guilt-ridden participants of the new order of "democracy" being established in France. This society created an underground system not unlike the underground railroad that later formed in the United States to bring southern slaves to the free states. This British-French secret alliance successfully saved the lives of dozens of wealthy French citizens.

On a mission to the north of France in 1793, Hickory Johnson I encountered a sight so disturbing that his recounting of the incident helped fuel the recruitment of many young men into the secret alliance. It was a story that so fascinated his grandson many years later that he gave the younger man a relic of great value to remember the incident by when young Hickory T Johnson III departed some twenty years later to set roots in America. The young man remembered well his grandfather's story of the strange young French nobleman who lay dead on the shores near St. Malo on the northern coast of France. His grandfather had just completed one of his clandestine trips to the north of France, crossing the English Channel on a private yacht, and making his way by skiff to the small island town jutting up out of the water just off of the coast. At low tide he set off to make his way across the sandy bridge to the mainland that would be submerged at high tide each day. When he reached the shores of the mainland early that morning, he happened upon the body of a young man who lay dead upon the beach in brightly colored, shiny underwear (or so presumed the young Brit). The dead man clasped an object close to his chest. A couple of hundred meters distant, smoke billowed from the burning wreck of the young man's carriage. It seemed rather large for a carriage, even for the carriage of a French nobleman, but it was in flames and too distant to see clearly.

His attention turned back to the young bourgeois gentleman. He pried loose the object that the dead man still clasped with surprising strength. It was a metallic object in the shape of an obelisk, which appeared to be made of a combination of precious metals, and had strange markings in what appeared to be a very precise pattern. Hickory T. Johnson I presumed it to be a family heirloom of such great importance that the poor lad cherished it above all else, grasping it tightly even in death.

After securing the object, he dragged the body off behind some bushes so it would not be found by the local Frenchmen who made their way across the bridge that nature created daily to connect St. Malo to the mainland. He then made his way to the burning wreck, but by the time he drew near enough to examine it, it had been consumed by the rising tide. The self-destruct mechanism that the time traveler in brightly-colored synthetic clothing had activated in his damaged starship was effective. When the tide receded, there was not a trace to be found.

Convinced that the time traveler was indeed a French nobleman who had fled when peasants attacked his carriage, Hickory Johnson I kept his scheduled encounter that day, and then returned to England with the body of the poor young man, in addition to a family of four that had been lucky enough to elude the new Parisian Guard. The young man could not be identified, and was buried in the Johnson family plot. The strange obelisk was given a place of distinction on the mantel over the immense fireplace in Johnson Manor, lending a sense of stark reality to the story that Hickory T Johnson III's grandfather would tell him through the years. Although he'd heard the story a hundred times before, it fascinated him anew each time. He was deeply honored to carry the obelisk with him to the New World.

Johnson landed in New York, but stopped only long enough to map out his travel plans. He was headed for Texas the minute he left London. Using his considerable wealth and a tenacious business sense, it took only a few years for him to establish one of the largest and most profitable cattle ranches in the territory. The obelisk took its place of prominence on the mantel at the Johnson ranch, always a reminder of his roots, and an inspiration to strive for what he believed in, just as his grandfather had taught him.

After a short time, Hickory Johnson faced a problem that most men only dream of: success came too easily. Cattle ranching wasn't the challenge he had thought it would be, the challenge he'd read about and longed for. Although it was an insurmountable challenge for most men, he was not most men. The business grew so fast that he spent his days in an office pushing papers to keep things organized while other men had the thrill he ached for in riding the range. He soon longed for a greater challenge, one that would lead him to rougher frontiers and a chance to try once again to conquer nature. The lure of California was irresistible. His fortune grew geometrically after he sold off his ranch and headed for the California territory.

The trip out was rugged, and while crossing the Arizona desert the wagon hit one of many large ruts. This one, however, would change Johnson's life. As the wagon bounced off the dusty trail and jolted back to the ground, a retainer strap broke loose, sending the luggage flying. They stopped to inspect the damage. Johnson, with two other passengers and the driver, climbed stiffly out of the wagon they'd been cramped into for the past several hours. They all stared in awe as they turned toward the bags strewn along the desert road, and were greeted by a rainbow of iridescence which spewed forth from the ground. They'd never seen anything like it. The driver dropped to his knees, sure he was facing his creator.

Johnson, who feared little and craved the unknown, walked slowly over to inspect the light. He was startled to discover that its source was the obelisk that had sat sedately on his family's mantel place for years. None of the bags were damaged except for one. The bag that had held the obelisk had burst open on impact with the road, though nothing had fallen out but the one bright object. Although he'd stared at it a thousand times before trying to decipher its significance, he'd never seen it exposed to the sunlight.

The bright desert sun reflected off of the contours of the shiny metal with an iridescence typical of vitanium, a viridium-titanium alloy, but of course none of these men had ever seen vitanium. It hadn't been discovered until hundreds of years after their deaths.

When Hickory T. Johnson settled in Arrowhead, the obelisk took its natural place on the mantel in his ranch. On quiet nights he would admire it as he always had, and feel comfort in its connection to the home of his youth and the family he cherished so far away. But it also stirred within him the excitement of his grandfather's stories, particularly the story of the French nobleman from whom it had come. He always felt that it had a greater purpose, that it was meant for a more exciting existence than collecting dust on the family's fireplace mantel, and the memory of the brilliant iridescence shining up from the desert road that day only reinforced that feeling each time he gazed upon it.

When his Wild West Show became a reality, the role of his treasured obelisk became clear. His most prized possession would be the beacon that would draw people to his new show. And so it did.

When the show first started, it drew only a local crowd. Although the performers were quite good, folks weren't interested in traveling through the desert just to see a couple of sharpshooters. But the obelisk was a different story. Once it was seen in public, word spread quickly of the magnificent light it spewed so brightly into the air that it could be seen a half-mile away by spectators approaching the arena. It wasn't until a few years later that the show itself became the main attraction, but even then the obelisk remained a drawing card that kept any other sharpshooter show from competing.

The lure of an object of the purest gold and silver known to man was, needless to say, a temptation to every outlaw in the West. Many thought of plotting to steal the obelisk, but none were willing to risk raiding an arena full of sharpshooters, or the infiltration of Arrowhead Ranch, where many of the show people lived and took turns guarding the Johnson house. But like almost everything in life, there's always an exception.

The Jensen Gang was a strange crew. Bill and Lil Jensen had built a reputation as some of the most clever raiders in the West before they burned down their cabin while in a drunken stupor. Their boys, Cal,

Hal and Al Jensen, were off on a job when the blaze had started. There were only ashes and bones by the time they returned home. In their horror, the boys vowed to continue the family business in honor of their departed parents. They had been well-trained by the famous duo, and decided to set their goals high. Lured by the stories of the obelisk, they plotted to get the youngest sibling, Al, into the show. He was a crack shot, and they were sure they'd have no trouble getting a foothold in Arrowhead.

Al was fifteen when he rode into Arrowhead, as cocky as most of the young men who came to join the show. And like most of the other young men, his skills were far below what he believed them to be. But unlike the other young men, he had a higher goal and the self-discipline to see it through. He charmed his way into the show as a stagehand, and quickly gained the friendship and trust of all who were around him.

Six months had passed since Al had joined the show. He was the stagehand who did the final preparation of the props just before they were taken into the arena to set up for each new performer. The only thing that would be between him and the obelisk at the Destin Fair were the two men assigned to guard the arena entrance and the obelisk. He had worked hard to gain the trust of the Johnsons, but hadn't quite been able to worm his way into being one of the guards yet. He knew it would just be a matter of time before he would get the opportunity to serve as one of the trusted guardians of the obelisk.

He tried hard to convince Cal and Hal as the Destin Spring Fair approached that this would not be the right time to make their move. He knew that he was gaining the confidence of the Johnsons and that eventually he would be in the position of having only one other guard to overcome to grab his treasure. He'd worked hard to get this far and didn't want to blow his chance. Unfortunately, his brothers had grown impatient. Without their parents, and with Al tied up with the show, times were tough. They hadn't been able to pull off a job in six months and money was getting tight. They wouldn't wait for the next fair. Al would be close enough to get them near the obelisk in Destin, and would be in position to distract the sharpshooters long enough for them to get away. They had confidence in their little brother's ability to fast-talk his way past any obstacles. They would make their move this year.

What they didn't expect was competition from a pair of time bandits.

CHAPTER XII

Plan B

Stryker and McGee rode back into town, this time making the trip a little more quickly. They were starting to get the hang of riding and didn't need as many breaks to survive the trip without their rear-ends going numb. They boarded their horses at the livery stable and headed for the ticket office at the Wild West Show.

"Whoever's got my six-shooter's probably already discovered that they can't miss with that thing. If it's somebody who's part of the show, they'll shoot better than they've ever shot in their life. If it's somebody who's not part of the show, they'll be the new star in Sunday's show. Hell, anybody who's settled in Arrowhead Canyon only came here because they wanted to be in the show. The first thing they'd do if they found that gun would be to try out for the show."

"Yeah!" T.C. exclaimed, catching on to Danny's logic. "Either way, whoever's got that gun'll stick out like a sore thumb."

"Right."

The two men stopped on the dusty landing in front of the Arrowhead ticket office, and stared up at the large plank over the widow with CLOSED written across it in bright red letters. This was usually the biggest ticket day of the week for advance sales to Sunday's show. The two men were dumbfounded.

"I don't like this, Danny. That hotel clerk said this show never closes. Something's not right here. Do you suppose some Teconean time travelers have beaten us to the obelisk?"

"Not likely. No one in the Teconean Empire stems from human ancestry. A Teconean wouldn't exactly go unnoticed around here."

"On the other hand, Teconean time travelers from our own future could have changed quite a bit from the Teconeans that we know. Pretty much anything's possible when you start messing with the space-time continuum."

The streets were unusually quiet, unlike the two men had ever seen before in Arrowhead.

"I don't have a good feeling about this either, buddy. Let's head back to the saloon. There's bound to be somebody there, and if anybody would know what's going on around town, it's probably the barkeeper."

Virgil Cooney was behind the bar in his saloon as usual, but the place was empty except for two men at a corner table, snoring away with their feet propped up and their empty mugs dangling loosely in their limp hands.

"Spring Fair time sure is bad for business," said Virgil, glad to see some sober customers to talk to.

"Spring Fair?" Danny muttered questioningly.

"Sure. You boys must be new to these parts."

"Yeah."

"Destin Spring Fair, second Sunday of every March. It's the only time the show ever travels anymore. Old man Johnson likes to honor his Belle by sending the show there for their Spring Fair every year."

"Oh!" the two nouveau cowboys said in unison smiling at each other.

"Well, I'm glad you boys are happy," Virgil smirked bitterly. "Business is dead. Pretty near every able-bodied citizen of Arrowhead works with that show and travels with it to Destin. And there sure as hell are no visitors to this dust bowl of a town when the show's gone. Hell, I think next year I'll just close up and take a vacation."

"Sorry, Virgil. We're just glad we'll still be able to see the show."

"Heh! The laugh's on you boys. The Destin Show's sold out a year in advance. If'n you get there quick enough, you might still be able to get tickets for next year's show. They start sellin' 'em as soon as the show starts, to give different people a chance to get the tickets next year. Oh, and don't think about tryin' to buy 'em off somebody who's already got 'em. There was some rough stuff a few years back with some town folks gettin' shot up cause they didn't want to sell, so the Sheriff don't allow no private ticket sellin' no more. About the only way to see that show is to sit up on the mountainside at the edge of town, but from a quarter mile away the view ain't too good. If I was you boys, I'd just hang out here and try and get a couple of good seats to next week's show. Besides, I'll sell you some cheap beers. Business is kind of slow."

"Thanks for the offer, Virgil," Danny said with a forced smile.

T.C. looked over at Danny. "So what's Plan B, Ace?"

"I'll let you know when I think of it."

"Ah well," said T.C. settling back on a barstool. "Two cold ones, Virgil. And give us the best table in the house."

CHAPTER XIII

The Destin Spring Fair

It was crisp clear morning. The sun perked up over the desert and lit the sky with a faint crimson glow as the first rays of morning touched the sand. It was a welcome sight to the people of Destin who were out their doors at the crack of dawn, eagerly getting ready for the show and their best business day of the year. Within minutes, the streets were bustling with activity as people industriously started their preparations, trying to beat the day's rapidly-building heat.

Destin had become a beautiful little town. It wasn't quite as opulent as Arrowhead, but it had a quaint, clean atmosphere that the hardworking townsfolk were proud of. One and two story wooden structures lined both sides of the wide Main Street that stretched east and west from the center of town. Most of the buildings were two story dwellings with various shops on the ground level and living quarters above, which opened onto balconies rimmed by whitewashed, carved railings. Each was neatly kept and joined with the adjacent buildings to create a continuous overhang that shaded the walkway below, which ran along the shops. Shopkeepers were scurrying to spruce up their window displays for the visitors who invariably spent their money more freely than the thrifty townspeople of Destin.

The westernmost end of Main Street was flagged on one side by the livery stable, and on the other by McCleary's General Store, the largest proprietorship in town after the saloon, the bank, and of course the Destin Inn. The Inn was far and away the largest building in town with its four story structure, but could house only a small percentage of the Spring Fair's patrons, many of whom would stay with local homeowners who were lucky enough to have an extra room to rent. The rest camped in the foothills of the mountains adjacent to town. The local ranchers were tolerant of squatters during Spring Fair week, but made it well known that no one should overstay their welcome.

Between the stable and McCleary's Store, a large banner hung over the entrance to Main Street. Strewn across the large white center band, flanked by red above and blue below, were the bold letters:

WELCOME
to the DESTIN SPRING FAIR
of 1849

The citizens of Destin were proud of the annual event that drew people from all over the territory. They were proud of their pristine town, known territory-wide for its law and order. It was a safe and quiet place to raise a family—an uncommon place in the wild West.

*   *   *   *   *   *   *   *

Danny and T.C. marveled at the quaint beauty of the town and the activity that bustled around it. It was a sharp contrast to their previous venture into Destin. Before the town had been spruced up for the Fair, it had been quaint and clean, but devoid of activity and its now-lively citizens had been dull and emotionless. The two men had decided that they might as well make the trip. If they were lucky, they might at least figure out who had the six-shooter, even if they couldn't get near the obelisk. Their horses trotted into town at midday, and they had little trouble getting a seat for lunch at the hotel restaurant, which had emptied as people with tickets made their way to the show.

After a quick meal, they mounted up and headed south from the town's center, veering off Main Street and down Arena Road, which ended a half-mile away at the arena, the site of the Spring Fair. They knew they couldn't get in, and they didn't see much point in sitting up on the adjacent bluff, too far to see any real action. Danny and T.C. figured their best bet would be to roam the fairgrounds and poke around for information.

CHAPTER XIV

The Chase

The Wild West Show was the centerpiece of the Destin Spring Fair. It was the reason that most people came to the fair, although the whole town was decked out for celebration. Along Arena Road the shopkeepers set up booths in front of their walkways selling anything they could interest visitors in. Stamped coins and painted rocks commemorating the show were adorned with the image of Hickory and Belle Johnson and marked with the date of the show. These were always a favorite of the kids lucky enough to have talked their parents into a trip to the fair. The scent of fresh baked goods wafted down the road, drawing folks in as they made their way into the fairgrounds.

The end of Arena Road was adorned with a banner similar to the one that greeted visitors at the entrance to Main Street. The bright red, white and blue banner was tied to the second story porch railings of buildings on either side of the road, and arched down toward the center at a gentle angle. As visitors strolled down the dusty road toward the fair, they were greeted by the boldly-colored banner and the sight of bustling crowds on the other side. Just beyond the banner was a grand central walkway, flanked on either side by the entrance to two small walkways fanning out in either direction.

The powerful scent of beef barbecuing in large pits drew the attention of most visitors down the road to the right as they entered, with the heat and billowing smoke not nearly enough of a deterrent to sway many from the whims of their stomachs. A small walkway led to an open field with rows and rows of wooden tables, each long enough to seat a small army, and grouped into four sections. At the entrance to each of these sections was a large barbecue pit manned by two Destinites, one diligently working the beef over the flames to assure that it was cooked to perfection, and the second doling out portions large enough to weigh down the heftiest of men. At either end of the pit were lemonade stands, where the women of Destin took turns pouring out what was reputed to be the best lemonade in the West. Actually, it was nothing special, but the excitement of the day combined with the heat of the BBQ pits made it awfully inviting. That, and the fact that the folks who waited in the long lines wanted to be able to say they'd tasted Destin lemonade, made for the inflated reputation the drink enjoyed.

Those family visitors whose taste buds weren't as strong as their kids' were pulled instead down the path to the left when they entered the fairgrounds. Here was the stuff that fairs were made of in the dreams of children. The path was lined on both sides with small stands full of children's trinkets that parents loathed, but usually agreed to buy anyway to quiet the cries of their youngsters. There were marbles and painted rocks, carved wooden Indians and horses, and of course toy guns carved of wood for those still too young for the real thing. A bit further along were games of skill—perhaps more accurately described as games of chance—little chance, such as tossing a rock into a basket too small to hold it, throwing rocks at wooden targets which never seemed to fall over, or, for the older children, the chance to shoot a .22 with a bent sight at a target that seldom had to be replaced for the next shooter. No matter how many people lost, the games always looked beatable to the next child in line. Scattered between the games were candy stands and fried dough vendors who covered their goods with enough sugar to tempt parents and children alike. The children were pulled to the various booths like magnets, but those with enough fortitude made it to the large clearing at the end and indulged in pony rides while their parents enjoyed some welcome tent shade and, of course, some of that most famous Destin lemonade. A good time was had by all.

Whether visitors circulated to the right or the left, all roads converged at the arena. The two side paths circled around and emptied back into the end of the large central walkway just outside the entrance to the arena, creating a traffic jam many tried to avoid by taking their seats early.

The large central walkway was a showpiece in and of itself. Stretching from the arched banner at the end of Arena Road to the entrance of the famous Wild West Show Arena was the central walkway. It was a large open path with a central island bordered by rocks protecting a staggered row of date palms, which provided little shade but lent a graceful elegance to the pathway. On either side of the island was a broad, sandy road full of people milling back and forth among the temporary shops set up along the rim of the path. By and large, these shops were manned by gunsmiths from all over the territory who converged on Destin each spring, gladly paying the exorbitant rent required to display their wares to the weekend crowds. They set up large booths, and each would try to outdo the others with extravagant decorations to lure the customers to their wares. The brisk weekend sales from this show could make or break a shopkeeper for the year. Many a gunsmith had made his name with a new pistol or rifle introduced at the fair, and would become renowned in the territory if the craftsmanship was good enough. Many of these shoppers were knowledgeable gunmen, and the quality had to be first rate to make the grade. A bad showing here had been known to end the career of more than a few aspiring gunsmiths.

In the middle of the central walkway, at a break in the island of palms, stood a small wooden structure adorned with a red, white, and blue ribbon that was draped from corner to corner of the roof on all four sides. Under the banners on three sides were large, hand-painted posters depicting Belle performing various feats for which she had become famous. On the fourth side, facing the arena, was a double-height door, the top half of which would open to become a ticket widow once the show had started. Those without tickets would begin to line up right after lunch to get their chance to purchase tickets for next year's show.

The show was scheduled to start at three o'clock, as the heat of the afternoon sun was just starting to break. By the second half of the show after intermission, the temperature would usually be quite pleasant, enhancing the enjoyment of the moment and helping to assure that all would go home happy. But when the gates opened at two o'clock, it was still brutally hot and the lines at the ticket booth for next year's show wrapped around the small building and stretched all the way back to the entrance under the great banner. Tempers intermittently flared as the crowd waited in the heat for the ticket booth to open. Those fortunate enough to have tickets for this year's show began milling into the arena as the doors opened, eager to find their seats and view the final preparations. The show started promptly at three with an action-packed grand opening, and those in line at the ticket booth looked up in envy at the arena as the explosion of oohs, ahs, and applause thundered out toward them. It somehow made the wait in line seem more palatable. At three-fifteen, the ticket booth opened, and the mood became distinctly more jovial as the line began to move at long last.

Danny and T.C. were enjoying the fair as much as anyone; probably more, in Danny's case, as he perused all the paraphernalia that he'd read about in wonder since his boyhood.

"I don't think we're making any progress here, Ace," T.C. muttered, as he fanned himself with his ten-gallon hat. In spite of all the appropriate garb, he still looked uncomfortably out of place, like a young athlete donning a tux for the first time at a formal charity ball.

"Yo, Ace!" he remarked a bit more emphatically, trying to get Danny's attention away from a target shooting demonstration at one of the gunsmith's booths.

"Yeah, O.K.," Danny snapped back as he reluctantly turned away from the booth. "I guess we'd better head around back behind the arena and see if we can get any closer. We're not going to get any info around here."

The two men headed out of the fairgrounds and back down Arena Road. They made their way to their horses, looked up in pain at the thought of remounting, painfully got on their horses and rode out of town to circle back behind the arena. By the time they made their way within eyeshot of the back entrance of the arena, it was four o'clock and the first half of the Show was drawing to a close.

As Billy D. headed out into the arena to close out the first half of the show, the backstage entrance area was quiet. All the other performers were relaxing in the performers' tent except for the few, including Belle, who wanted to see Billy's long-awaited debut at the fair. Al was alone except for the two guards who had taken seats just inside the arena entrance to watch Billy perform. Al casually made his way to the backstage entrance and gave the all clear signal to his brothers, who were waiting a short distance away with their saddled horses nearby.

Cal and Hal made their way into the staging area while their brother darted into an adjacent room to avert suspicion. The two men had no trouble sneaking up behind the guards who were sitting on either side of the obelisk stand. They hit the two men simultaneously in the backs of their heads with the butts of their guns, grabbed the obelisk, and darted through the staging area to their waiting horses. They were galloping along the foothills toward a nearby canyon entrance before anyone realized what was going on.

By the time the screams for help started from the nearby spectators, Billy was the only one with a horse. Everyone else in the show had completed their first-half performances, and their horses had been unsaddled and were being brushed down and rested in preparation for the second half of the show. The brothers were well on their way before anyone got Billy's attention. Once Al was sure that his brothers were well clear of the arena and that the screams for help already had started, he ran out into the arena, and played his part well. He looked as horrified as anyone in the area at the sight of the two bleeding guards and the missing obelisk. He joined the group that was yelling for Billy.

Billy was absorbed in his performance, and basking in the moment of glory that he had awaited for so long. It took a few moments to get his attention, but once he realized what had happened, he galloped straight through the staging area and started after the Jensens. With his newfound confidence, he paid no attention to the fact that he was alone.

Al had his horse saddled quickly and was only a few paces behind Billy as the chase began. He and Billy followed the trail of dust that was kicked up by the Jensens' horses. They had little trouble keeping pace but were slow to make up ground.

"Hello. That looks interesting," muttered Danny.

T.C. turned to see the two pairs of horsemen in the distance, turning at a full gallop into the canyon road as throngs of people came running out the back of the arena yelling something about the stolen obelisk. "Could be Plan B, buddy."

Stryker and McGee took off at a full gallop to join in the chase, as everyone else scrambled hopelessly for their horses, none of which would be saddled up before the men were well into the canyon.

Billy galloped headlong after the two bandits who had robbed the show. The desert sun beat down on him and the sweat poured off his brow, blurring his vision as it seeped into his eyes. He fought to stay focused, riding after the criminals with a reckless abandon that characterized the arrogant gunmen of the West whose ranks he had recently joined since finding the six-shooter. The steadily pounding cadence of the iron horseshoes against the hard desert floor made him oblivious to the rider who had joined in his chase with gun drawn and ready to shoot Billy down if the sharpshooter took aim at his brothers. Billy D. was focused on the dust clouds that swirled up from the hooves of the

Jensens' horses, and strained to see the men he was chasing though the canyon.

Cal and Hal were keenly aware of the relentless pursuit of the two horsemen, taking some solace in knowing that the second one should be their little brother, if he kept to the plan. About a mile into the canyon, they turned into a small winding pathway that led up and around a rock formation into an easily defensible bluff with a back road out to the adjacent canyon; this was a little-traveled route to the San Francisco road. Everything was going according to plan. *Ma and Pa would be proud*, Cal thought as they quickly rounded the rock formation and dismounted.

Billy remained in close pursuit. He didn't have much experience at this, and didn't bother thinking ahead. He darted up the winding canyon pathway and rounded the rock formation that hid the clearing where the Jensens were waiting. He fell off his horse as the pain singed his arm. He hit the ground before the sound of the shot registered and he realized that the pain was coming from a bullet that had torn its way through his left biceps. In a reflex of self-preservation, he leapt behind the rock formation that guarded the entrance to the bluff.

"What the hell am I doing?" he muttered to himself, as the reality of the moment set in.

"Hey, Billy!"

He turned quickly at the unexpected greeting, and was relieved to see help as Al rode up behind him and dismounted. Like most of the performers in the show, Billy had taken to Al quickly, and the two had become good friends over the past six months. Or so he thought.

"What are we going to do now? Is anyone else with you?"

"It's just you and me, friend. And what you're going to do is unholster that six-shooter with your left hand very slowly and toss it out there," said Al with a wry smile, motioning for Billy to toss his gun out into the clearing.

Billy was stunned. He was rarely at a loss for words, but this was one of those times.

"Let's do it, friend!" Al snapped, the smile vanishing from his face as he raised his gun toward Billy.

Billy winced, the pain shooting through him like a red-hot poker as he lifted his wounded left arm to unholster the gun.

"Now!" yelled Al with a ferocity Billy had never seen in him. Al knew a posse would be arriving soon, and was anxious to get Destin well behind him. Too many people knew his face now.

Billy painfully tossed his six-shooter a short distance past the rocky bluff, then forlornly slumped back against the rocks.

"Let's move it, cowboy."

Al was relieved to see the six-shooter out of the reach of the man he'd seen fire a round of five dead-center through pennies at twenty paces. He coaxed Billy up, and led him out into the bluff to greet his brothers.

Hal smiled. "Good job, little bro."

Billy stared at his turncoat friend in disbelief, only now realizing what was going on. "You were in this from the start?" he sighed in disbelief.

"What are we gonna do with this guy now?" asked Cal, as they all ignored the question of their unwanted prisoner. "You were supposed to shoot him in the back, little bro."

Al glanced up with a look of horror on his face. "Ma and Pa taught us better than that, Cal. There ain't no dignity in shootin' a man in the back."

"You done pretty good up until now, but maybe you just ain't got the stomach for this line of work, little bro," said Hal as he drew his gun toward Billy. "I guess I'll just have to finish your job for you."

Billy's eyes bulged out of their sockets as Hal lifted his pistol. With a steely glint of pleasure, he slowly lifted the revolver toward Billy at point blank range, enjoying the animal-like panic of his victim.

"Hell! You're sick, Hal," Cal snapped. "Give the man a little dignity. Get it over with."

As Hal turned to glare at his brother a shot rang out behind them and the three men spun and turned as a rockslide thundered down the ridge. Billy jumped back and fell as he turned to run to his horse. As he fell to the ground he saw the blurred image of Danny Stryker lunging for the six-shooter. Before the three Jensen brothers realized what was going on, Danny had loaded the silver bullet and trained his gun on the Jensens. All three of them fell simultaneously from the wide-burst phased sonic pulse emanating from the six-shooter as the sound of a single shot rang out.

Billy's jaw dropped as his gaze went from Danny to the three limp bodies, and then back to Danny again.

"Damn! You're better with that thing than I am."

"That's because it's mine. I lost it a couple of days ago."

Billy knew the man was right, and that his life would never be the same again. Nonetheless, he was relieved to be alive.

After creating the rockslide diversion, T. C. grabbed his saddlebag and headed for the Jensens' horses. In his bag was a replica of the obelisk, exact in size and scale but totally nonfunctional as an FDS core module, and crafted of gold and silver rather than vitanium. It was still quite a treasure, monetarily speaking, but would have no technological impact on history if left in 1849. He stealthily exchanged it for the real obelisk stashed in Cal Jensen's saddlebag and handed the bag to Billy.

Billy stood as Danny finished applying a pressure bandage to his wound. He stared in disbelief as he reached in the saddlebag and pulled out the obelisk.

"Why are you guys giving this to me? You're the heroes."

"We've got someplace else we've got to be in a hurry, friend," said Danny, as he finished tying the Jensen brothers together. "You can be the hero."

And he was. Billy was waiting alone with the obelisk in hand and the Jensen gang in knots as the posse from Destin finally made its way into the canyon.

"Been waitin' for you boys," he said with a wry smile as the posse rode in.

He never could shoot quite the same after that, but he was famous nonetheless for single-handedly capturing the Jensen gang and recovering the obelisk. It never reflected the light quite as brightly after that day, but everyone just figured it had gotten tarnished in the scuffle. Even though Billy was no longer a sharpshooter, he never lost his confidence. He continued to grow with the Wild West Show and developed keen business acumen. When Hickory died a few years later, Billy took over management of the show for Belle. He developed it into a series of spectacular groups of performers that were based in cities throughout the West. He even started an annual tour of the east coast cities that cemented his fame in American history.

The Life and Times of Billy Delaney was published by a reporter from Baltimore in 1899.

CHAPTER XV

Back to the Future

Stryker and McGee headed out the back road of the canyon bluff, leaving Billy behind just moments before the posse arrived. Billy was only too glad to take the credit, and kept Stryker and McGee's secret safe for the rest of his life.

It was about an hour's ride back to the ship through the canyon roads that Danny and T.C. were getting to know too well. They were anxious to get back to the comforts of the twenty-fifth century. Even Danny had had his fill of nostalgia and was ready to make the time jump. As they trotted up the narrow canyon to the hiding place of the Stargazer, they felt the low rumble of the engines. Beck darted out of the camouflaged landing where the ship was hidden as the men turned the corner.

"I've been monitoring the location of the obelisk. I saw you closing in and prepped the ship for take-off. You being followed?"

Danny glanced back over his shoulder. "I don't think so, but we'd better get going before somebody starts looking."

"Let's get off this rock. I'm going out of my mind cooped up in this ship," said Beck, with the first hint of emotion that confirmed that he might actually be human after all.

Danny and T.C. unsaddled their horses. They knew they could not bring anything back to the future that was not meant to be there, but what could a couple of saddles and a few nick-knacks hurt. They found it surprisingly hard to part with the horses, but knew the steeds would find their way back to town and to a grateful new owner.

Once inside the Stargazer, they quickly reacclimated to the luxury of conditioned air, something they would never take for granted again. Danny and T.C. fastened into their seats, and within seconds Beck had guided them out of Earth's atmosphere. As the ship ascended, it accelerated too rapidly for anyone on the ground to focus on, but the bright glint reflecting off the craft caught Billy's eye. He just figured God was winking at him.

*   *   *   *   *   *   *   *

As soon as The Stargazer achieved orbit, Danny and T.C. released their seat restraints and headed back to their quarters. It would take about fifteen minutes for Beck to plot the time-warp coordinates into the computer to calculate a safe jump, and Danny and T.C. couldn't get to the decontamination units (DC's) fast enough. Danny usually hated the DC's that were found on Space Corps vessels. The fine-mist water conservation systems could never compare with a good hot shower, Danny had always said, but compared to Destin's washtubs even a DC would feel great. They couldn't wait to get the desert dust out from under their skin.

After a quick but almost satisfying "shower," Stryker headed down the short corridor to the bridge. As he turned the corner, he winced and instinctively grabbed for his knee before even realizing the sensation of searing pain that had struck him. Before his hand could reach its target, Danny fell to the ground in pain, and as he leaned against the burnished steel walls, his gaze focused on Beck, who stood facing him with an electromagnetic-pulse emitter aimed directly at him.

"Don't make me fire again, Stryker," he said sternly.

They both turned their heads toward the click of the door that came from T.C.'s quarters.

"Get back!" Danny shouted.

T.C., who had just emerged from the doorway, spun quickly back toward his room at the sound of Danny's voice, but Beck's aim was too quick. T.C. shrieked in pain and there was a loud thud as his body hit the floor.

"Ahh! I can't feel my legs."

Beck's shot had hit him squarely on the spine between the eleventh and twelfth thoracic vertebrae. The EM-pulse wave struck the spinal cord, and the resulting disruption of neural impulses had induced an immediate spinal cord injury.

"You're lucky," Beck quipped. "It's only an EM-pulse. You'll regain full function within a couple of hours. In the meantime, you two will be out of my way."

"What the hell's going on here?" a confused T.C. asked painfully, still feeling the searing sensation typical of the EM-pulse weapon that had so effectively struck his back.

"Don't be so surprised, buddy," Danny said. "I told you I never trusted this guy. Obviously, he's the mole who's been supplying tech information to the Teconeans."

"Shut up and help your friend into a chair," Beck ordered.

Stryker struggled against his painful knee and dragged his partner's massive body into the chair, then fastened the safety harness.

"Sit down and enjoy the show, Stryker."

Danny complied, not wanting to challenge a charged EM-pulse emitter. He sat down in the seat next to T.C. and applied his own harness as well, still feeling wobbly from the knee pain and the effort of dragging his bulky friend into the chair. He glared at Beck, who fired again, striking Danny's right arm.

"What the hell was that for?" he shrieked painfully, trying to massage out the pain with his left hand.

"Just in case you had any ideas of getting ambitious. I don't need any heroes complicating my life right now." Beck set down the emitter and picked up a hand phaser.

"Whoa!" said Danny. "Are you nuts? What can we possibly do in this position? My right arm's a noodle, my leg will barely hold me up, and T.C.'s a para."

Beck sneered. "Just in case," he said as he raised his phaser in T.C.'s direction.

"No!" Danny yelled.

Beck fired at the harness buckle and fused it shut. "I'm not a monster," he laughed, as he fired again to fuse Stryker's buckle. Danny and T.C. exhaled audibly and sunk in their chairs. "I'll cut you out when we arrive. Your neural function will have returned to normal by then."

"Arrive where?" T.C. asked.

"Tri-Luna," Danny cut in before Beck could respond.

"Very good, hero," he mused. "Enjoy the ride."

CHAPTER XVI

The Birth of the Empire

484 years earlier—Summer, 2013

The light of day crept over the encampment at the base of the Himalayan range where this summer's expedition was to take place. The rays of the warm morning sun began to burn off patches of the fog that hung between the vast mountain peaks. This was Professor Smithson's favorite part of his famous summer excursions. The groundwork was all done and only the excitement of exploration lay ahead. As the bacon sizzled in the frying pan that he had placed over the campfire, the inhabitants of three adjacent tents began to stir. There was nothing like the smell of bacon wafting through the crisp morning air to motivate a camper to crawl out of his cozy cocoon of a sleeping bag. The women were the first to emerge, feeling the instinctively nurturing urge to relieve their professor of such a mundane task.

"Don't be so sexist, Miss Parker," he laughed as Sara Parker and Jeannie Jackson approached the fire. They felt a bit foolish and giggled nervously as they settled in on the smooth rocks next to the professor.

"That smells great," came a yawn-strained voice from behind them. They all turned and laughed again at the visage of Jason's disheveled head poking through the tent door. "Aw, shoot," he muttered as he struggled to regain his grasp on the tent flaps that he had been holding together to protect his vanity. Jason Langley was the captain of the Boston University football team and valedictorian of the B.U. Class of

2013. He was bred of upper crust ancestry from one of New England's wealthiest families, and although he strove to be the picture of nonchalance to blend in with his classmates, his finely-bred manner awkwardly shone through. His appearance was always immaculate, with every hair in place, and highlighted his ruggedly handsome and sharply cut facial features. As he heard the laughs, he quickly retreated back into the tent in a self-conscious state of near panic and began to comb the thick dark hair that sprawled haphazardly from his head. *This is going to be a long trip*, he thought. A few moments later the four boys who occupied the two remaining tents joined the trio and pitched in to finish preparing breakfast.

The spring semester at B.U. had ended only one week earlier. The summer expedition with Professor Smithson was the most sought-after activity on campus. James Smithson had been a highly decorated Air Force captain who took early retirement due to an inner ear problem that caused intermittent vertigo and rendered him unsafe to fly at the age of thirty-six. He had taken a job as a professor of Botany at B.U., where his zest for teaching and engaging the imagination of students had earned him the reputation of most popular teacher on campus—even though it *was* Botany he taught. Each summer he led a one-week nature expedition, each time to a different but equally-exciting, isolated location. For these forays, he would choose six of his brightest and most energetic students to join him, trying to satisfy his desire for teaching at the highest possible level. These adventures had become legendary among B.U. students, and hundreds of matriculating seniors would apply each year, hoping to cap off their college career with a Smithson Expedition.

This year, the expedition led off the summer of '13 with a trip to a remote section of the Himalayas. The plan was not to ascend the mountain, a task that Smithson generally avoided due to his propensity for vertigo, but rather to explore the rich vegetation of one of the foothill valleys. They had flown from Logan Airport to Heathrow, and from there caught the redeye to Katmandu. They had arrived shortly after sunrise and were met at the airport by the helicopter guide Smithson had hired through his university contacts. After a breakfast and bathroom break, the tired but eager group had loaded onto the chopper. They had traversed the one hundred and twenty miles to the pristine valley that Smithson had charted. Much of the flatlands of Nepal had been ravaged by deforestation in the late twentieth century, and Smithson had picked this spot carefully. It was still untouched by human development—a model of the beauty that the raw forces of nature had created over the millennia. After a day of hiking through the dense forest, they had set up camp at the base of a vast peak that marked the beginning of the mountain range. Thoroughly exhausted, the explorers had dragged their aching bodies into their tents and had fallen into a sound sleep shortly after dusk.

James Smithson and his six students finished breakfast and broke camp early, eager to get on with their adventure. Jason excused himself from the rest of the group and headed into the thick brush with a roll of toilet paper tucked under his arm.

"Time to provide some fresh fertilizer to the jungle."

The group laughed, and turned back to the task of breaking down camp. They would leave a storage tent and whatever supplies they could do without for the next few days of the journey.

"Pack light," Smithson reminded his students. "We're likely to encounter some rugged terrain along the way. The less you're carrying, the easier the trek will be."

The sun was already getting hot, and the novice explorers were tiring of all of the tedious preparation and anxious to be on their way. They turned in unison toward a rustling in the underbrush. The sound seemed to be racing toward them. Smithson quickly drew and steadied his rifle.

"Professor!" rang out a breathless voice, as Jason's body emerged from the thicket in front of them. "You've got…to see this!…I stum…."

"Slow down, Jason," Smithson replied as they all let out a sigh of relief. Wildlife was reported to be sparse in the area, but young imaginations are vivid, especially when fueled by other young imaginations. "Is there something following you? Are you in danger?"

"What?" Jason asked with a perplexed look on his face. His face relaxed and broadened into a smile as he realized the spectacle that he must have created dashing out from the thick underbrush. "No, no. It's not that," he said anxiously.

"What is it then, Jason? Slow down and tell us what you saw."

"Yeah," Sara said with a bit of disgust in her voice. "Keep your pants on." She was embarrassed at how easily she had been frightened, and hoped none of the others had noticed. They hadn't, of course, since they had all been equally terrified at the prospect of seeing their first predator in the wild. But Sara was very proud and refused to rely on others, either physically or emotionally. She worked hard at maintaining an image of fierce independence.

Jason glanced nervously down, so excited at that moment that he wasn't sure whether he'd forgotten to pull up his pants before he dashed out into the open. He looked up sheepishly. They all laughed and looked over at Sara.

"Just an expression!" she blurted, as she felt the warm blush rise up into her cheeks.

"What is it, Jason?" the professor interrupted, anxious to know what had startled his usually calm and collected star athlete. "What did you see?"

The excitement returned to Jason's voice. "A cave opening, Professor, with dark red and black wall paintings, showing a long line of people walking through an archway. Above the arch is the sun with its rays shining down and lighting the way into the arch."

"Very interesting, Jason," the professor began to respond. "I don't think these types of cave drawings have been described in this part of the world before. Has any one of you heard of…"

"No, no, Professor," Jason interrupted, "you don't understand. The people in the drawing aren't humans!"

Everyone's eyebrows rose simultaneously.

"Damn it, Jason. This is no time for one of your pranks," Deke Jackson said as he wiped sweat from his forehead with the back of his hand. "It's hot as hell and we all wanna get going."

Deke had known Jason since high school, and they were the best of friends. They considered themselves lucky to be tent-mates for this trip. He didn't mind putting Jason in his place when he felt he needed to, and he was just saying what they all felt. Jason was well known for his pranks on campus. They all began to turn away and resume their journey.

"No, wait, Deke," Jason said in an exasperated voice, and then looked over at Smithson again. "Professor, you've got to see this."

They continued to secure their packs.

"They *weren't* human figures. At least not *Homo sapiens sapiens*. The men in the drawing all had long arms and thick, powerful legs. Their faces were broad, with prominent chins."

Smithson stopped and turned to look up at Jason.

"Although the drawing is faded, parts of it are still real clear. I recognize the figures from my anthropology class…they're .."

"Neanderthals," Smithson completed Jason's sentence.

"Yeah, Professor. I'm sure of it."

"Fascinating," Smithson mused in a barely-audible mutter. "Here in the Himilayas?"

"And some of the drawings are in pristine condition," Jason continued. "It looks like a huge tree was recently uprooted from soil erosion and exposed the mouth of the cave. This tree is massive. The base must be thirty feet high. That's what drew my attention to it. It was growing right in front of the cave entrance. It must have been blocking it for decades. I doubt if anyone's been through that cave in at least a century; no one to disturb it."

"Well, ladies and gentlemen," the professor smiled, "the adventure begins."

"All right!" yelled Deke. "This is what I signed on for."

"This time," Smithson continued, glaring at Jason "let's all remember to travel in pairs at *all* times. And don't forget to carry your radios."

Jason's sheepish look turned to one of pride as the professor said, "Lead the way, Mr. Langley."

The seven explorers made their way to the cave entrance. They briefly stopped to marvel at the size of the uprooted tree near the cave opening. The entanglement of massive roots shot up nearly ten yards into the air and threw a magnificent maze of shadows across their path, providing some welcome shelter from the heat of the ever-increasing sunshine. The entrance was a perfectly-shaped archway that stood out from the mountainside like a fresco carved by mother nature, or perhaps, thought the professor, by the artisans of another era who had passed this way before. As the group stood admiring the sight, the sun crept up over the shade of the tree base, and bathed the arch in light.

"The drawing," Jason said. "It's the cave drawing—the archway with the sun overhead. Come on."

The seven explorers followed Jason into the entrance of the cave. The passageway through the arch was narrow and they had to file through in pairs. Twenty feet past the entry, the cave opened up into a cavern about twenty by thirty feet. It glowed a crimson hue with the reflected light that entered, but it retained a refreshing coolness throughout. Jason led them over to the left wall of the cavern. It was nearly covered with a detailed mural depicting a line of Neanderthals queued up to enter the archway two by two. Above the archway, as Jason had described, was a picture of the sun with its rays beaming down to light up the entrance to this cavern.

"The detail of this drawing is astounding," Smithson remarked. "We've known from archeological findings that the Neanderthals were somewhat advanced socially. Evidence of the remains of the elderly and disabled among them indicate that the younger and healthier Neanderthals cared for family or tribal members. But this depicts a much more organized and advanced culture than we had imagined. These drawings are the first that I know of to be discovered that are clearly Neanderthal. The detail indicates a far greater development of fine motor and perceptual skills than have been previously attributed to them. Look at how the picture is drawn with the figures ranging in size progressively to create three-dimensional perspective. Modern man, our *Homo sapiens sapiens* predecessors, didn't develop these skills until centuries later."

"What is most intriguing, however," he continued, "is the thought of what this drawing actually represents. Any ideas, ladies and gentlemen?"

"Freedom, I'd guess," piped in Deke. "The sun lighting the way would represent freedom to me."

"Freedom from what?" asked one of the other students. "The planet wasn't exactly overcrowded with slave dealers a hundred million years ago."

"Indeed," the professor answered. "But they were hardly the sole inhabitants of Earth. And it was hardly a hundred million years ago. *Homo sapiens neanderthalis* existed between about 130,000 and 40,000 B.C.. They inhabited parts of Europe and thrived among the less intelligent wildlife. Some anthropologists believe they represent a separate branch of evolution from our ancestors, *Homo sapiens sapiens*. They were a similarly-evolved people in many ways. We surmise from the size and shape of their skeletal remains that *Homo sapiens sapiens* were less powerful than the Neanderthals; however, the Neanderthals were less advanced in the use of tools and were thought to be less intelligent. It is believed by some that *Homo sapiens sapiens* originated in Africa and migrated up the African continent into Europe, where they coexisted with the Neanderthals for a period of time. At this point, history becomes even more blurry. We know that the Neanderthals ceased to exist around 40,000 years ago, but we don't know why. There are three major theories as to what happened to them."

"The first is that they evolved along similar paths into the humans that inhabit Earth today. This seems somewhat unlikely to me—that they would develop from a structurally different form of *Homo sapiens* into identical beings seems improbable."

"The second theory is more plausible. The thinking here is that when the two groups met, they coexisted in the same territory. They eventually interbred and melded the two gene pools into one. Although this is certainly possible, human nature also makes this one doubtful to me. Humans are very territorial, and notoriously unaccepting of anyone who looks different. Throughout modern history, racism always seems to rear its ugliness when a new culture seeps into a homogeneous society. It is only through the homogenization of cultural diversity that a new people are accepted. Only after the destruction of the very diversity that enriches and strengthens a society, are new people accepted. Only after those new people are no longer different."

"Then wouldn't this theory make a lot of sense?" Sara asked. "I mean, it would kind of mirror what happened in the United States in the twentieth century."

"Yes," Smithson replied "but those changes only occurred due to political pressure built on the modern consciousness that can subdue, but not destroy, the human instinct. Those political pressures did not exist 40,000 years ago. This is why I think that the third explanation is most likely."

"The third theory is that when the Neanderthals met our predecessors, instinct prevailed. Instinct to defend territory, defend their women, destroy those who had the gall to be different. Fierce fighting likely ensued. The Neanderthals were unmatched by any other foe our ancestors had encountered. They were their equals in many ways, and far more powerful physically. The war likely lasted for decades, or perhaps centuries. But in the end *Homo sapiens neanderthalis* succumbed to *Homo sapiens sapiens*. I suspect this was due to the advanced technology, which gave our ancestors superior weapons, probably a more highly-evolved intellect, and greater quickness derived from their body structures that provided the strategic edge necessary to overcome their disadvantage in sheer strength. In the end, Neanderthals became extinct. We destroyed another native endangered species on our planet."

"Freedom!" exclaimed Sara.

Everyone looked over at her, breaking away from the mural and its interpreter.

"That's what you meant. This cave and the sun that revealed its entrance to the Neanderthals represented freedom to them. It must have provided a safe haven for a group of Neanderthals fleeing from their enemies."

"Exactly, Miss Parker."

"But, Professor," Jason broke in, "I didn't think any Neanderthals lived in the Himalayas."

"Neither did the history books, Jason. But judging from this picture, many of them must have passed this way."

"Five hundred and eighty-four," Deke said.

The group glanced over at him.

"I counted 'em," he said proudly.

"And from the detail of this drawing, I would guess that was not a random number chosen by the artist. In fact, I doubt that this was considered art. Not as *we* know art, anyway. This was not drawn for decoration. It was drawn to tell a story, to record history. It is, in essence, the history book of these people," he said pointing to the figures on the wall. "And if we can find proof of that history, find the remains of Neanderthals here, we can add a new chapter to our own history books. As I said, ladies and gents, the adventure begins."

At the far end of the cavern was an opening seven feet high and six feet wide. It was the only exit from the cavern other than the one they had entered by, and the seven explorers made their way through the opening, which led to a tortuous cave. Little of the reflected sunlight of the cavern made its way into the cave, and what little light there was quickly dissipated with each turn of the cave walls. Sara and Jason led the way through the narrow passage vying playfully for the lead position, each determined to be the first to see whatever fascination lay ahead. The rest of the crew followed in single file, with Smithson in the rear keeping a watchful eye out for the safety of his students. They used their flashlights to light the way, which had become pitch black by the fourth turn, approximately one hundred yards into the cave. The path was fine gravel, and provided an audible trail that Smithson could follow as easily as the wavering flashlights. The cave walls were a cool, smooth, whitish-gray, reflecting enough light to allow them to find their way comfortably through the passage, which maintained fairly uniform dimensions throughout the walk. A faint rumble could be heard in the background, a noise that Smithson surmised must be emanating from underground rivers flowing through the mountain.

Jason came around the sixth turn in the cave and stopped. He peered ahead and turned off his light.

"Turn it off, Sara."

"Why, do you want to tell ghost stories?" she quipped. "I don't scare that easily."

"Turn it off, Sara. Look."

She turned off her flashlight and noticed a faint light up ahead.

"It's getting lighter again."

"We must be getting near the end," Jason said as he took off ahead of Sara.

"Hold up, you rat!"

The tunnel brightened as they continued through a series of turns. They were each so eager to get to the end first that they hardly noticed the increasing rumble of noise as they proceeded. Sara caught up to Jason, who was stopped at another twist in the cavern walls.

"What're you scared of, jocko?"

"Looks awful small," said Jason, looking ahead as the cave narrowed to a three-by-three-foot opening.

"See ya," Sara said as she darted into the small opening. She crawled on her hands and knees along the gravel path, now well lit by the light at the end of the tunnel. The roaring sound ahead became almost deafening. With each movement forward the sound became louder and Sara became more frightened, but there was no way she would admit it to Jason. She moved ahead at a slow but steady pace. As she reached the end of the passage, she noticed that the cave opened up into another chamber. This one appeared much more narrow that the one they had entered by. She peered at the facing rock wall only eight to ten feet away. The noise was quite loud now, but the cavern looked clear. Sara stepped out cautiously. The cavern was about fifteen feet high and opened to her right where the far wall was about twenty feet away and was lit from the left. *Must be the way out*, she thought. To her left was another rock face. There was only one way to go, and Sara slowly made her way to the right. Ten steps down the path she looked to her left and stopped, gaping in awe at a massive waterfall outside the cave that totally obliterated the exit.

Sara stared in awe at the power of the waterfall that tumbled from far above and plunged in a torrent to an unknown distance below. The gravel path pitched down toward the opening at a thirty-degree angle, and Sara began to think that their adventure was about to come to a sudden and disappointing end. She began to turn to look for Jason.

The rush of water was so loud that she hadn't heard Jason's approaching footsteps. Realizing that she was totally unaware that he was right behind her, Jason couldn't resist the temptation as Sara, now only inches away turned to look for him.

"Boo!" he shouted.

"Ahh!" she screeched to his delight. She jumped back, and her foot landed in the soft gravel at the top of the incline that led sharply down into the rushing waterfall. She tried desperately to regain her balance, but the path was so slick that she lost her footing. Her body struck the ground with a thud, and she winced at the pain of the gravel scraping up against her right cheek.

"Jason!" she screamed as she slid helplessly toward the waterfall. "Hel..."

Jason lunged forward, but could barely react before she was gone. Sara's voiced vanished completely as she was swallowed up by the roaring water. He was still standing there, staring in horror at the raging torrent when the rest of the group walked up behind him.

"Sara!" Smithson shouted, trying to be heard over the roar. "Where's Sara?"

Jason just stared ahead numbly.

"My God," Smithson whispered under his breath realizing what had just happened. "My God," he repeated to himself. A sickening feeling came over him. *I never should have let them get that far ahead,* he thought. *I should have known better. Maybe I'm losing my edge.*

"I'm going after her," Jason snapped, coming out of his horrified daze. "It was my fault. I'm going in after her."

"No," Smithson said, his leadership skills taking over instinctively. "First thing is to try and make radio contact with her. Turn around, Deke." He unzipped the lower pouch in Deke's backpack and pulled out the radio. The radios were single frequency walky-talky-type equipment that required no adjustments. "Sara, can you hear me? Come in, Sara. Over." He released the talk button. They all listened anxiously to the monotone of static. "Sara, are you O.K.?"

"Maybe she just hasn't had a chance to get it out of her pack yet, Professor."

"Maybe," Smithson answered. He had checked everyone's radios and made sure they were on and loud enough to hear before they had started into the cave. The packs were all designed to be watertight, so the radio wouldn't be damaged by the waterfall, but it would still take time to get to a dry area, remove the radio and answer. He waited anxiously.

"Professor!" urged Jason. "We can't keep waiting. Her pack could be pulling her under the water. She could be drowning!" He started to remove his pack and move toward the water.

"Hold it, Jason. Calm down and listen. You don't rush blindly into things out here. Think things through or you'll get yourself in trouble and won't be able to help Sara. Remember what I told you about these packs. They were designed for water safety. That's one reason your parents complained about how much they cost. Now you'll see why they paid it. The packs are watertight, and equipped with a water-sensing system. There's a small reservoir under the bottom of the pack angled to keep out water from above. The rain won't affect it, but if it submerges, the reservoir fills and triggers two compressed air canisters that fill bladders built into the front straps. It's a life vest that will keep you and your pack floating—face up.

"Sara!" he called again into the radio. Still he was answered by nothing but static. "That's it. I'm going in. Maybe she just hasn't gotten to her radio. But then again, maybe she can't. If you don't hear from me within fifteen minutes, head back to base camp and radio for help. I've got to get down there before she's too far away. This most likely leads to some sort of river." He handed Deke back his radio and secured his own pack.

"Yeah, but it could just plunge into the side of the mountain."

"Yup. Sure could," Smithson said as he jumped feet first into the glistening cascade. His leap was abruptly halted by the tremendous force of the water pushing him downward. The sudden impact knocked the breath out of him, and he fought to hold on to the little air left in his lungs. The drop was surprisingly quick. The icy cold water enveloped his body as he was pulled under the river by the force of his fall. The downward force created as the waterfall cut through the surface of the river dragged him further under, and he fought to get out of the downdraft. He was well trained and resisted the instinct to swim straight up until he had propelled himself free of the downdraft of water. It was like a rip-tide effect—if he swam against the current he would fatigue and drown, but if he broke out of the current first, his strength would propel him in the direction he wanted to go. He felt the downdraft pressure abate as he swam forward. He struggled against the urge to breathe in as his body craved fresh oxygen. His consciousness began to fog as he felt the straps of his pack tighten around him. The air bladders in the straps inflated quickly, propelling him to the surface. He instinctively gasped the fresh air as his head popped up out of the water.

As consciousness returned, Smithson realized that he was being pulled down river by a swift current carrying him away from the waterfall and toward the valley ahead. He could barely focus on the massive rocks that bounced his body around as the river propelled him forward. He fought to keep his feet pointed down river. The rapid flow of the water, which knew its way around the smooth boulders, guided his body safely with only minor bumps along the way. He struggled to look for any signs of Sara, but it was hard to gain any kind of vantage point in the water. He spotted an overhanging branch up ahead and guided his body, as best as he could, toward the spot. He lunged as he shot by and his body jerked up out of the water as he hooked the branch.

James Smithson pulled himself up, and managed to balance on top of a fork in the branch. His head hung down as he sat motionless except for his heaving chest, fighting to replenish his body's supply of oxygen. His respiration slowed after a few minutes, and he began to regain his composure. For the first time he realized where he was. He looked back at the waterfall about a half-mile upriver. It started about a quarter-mile up the side of the mountain and plunged forcefully down, cutting a path though the rock and creating two sheer cliffs about twenty feet in height on either side as it entered the river. The cave from which he had

entered the waterfall was camouflaged behind it, but Smithson surmised it must have started just above those cliffs. The fall had been
short. His eyes traced the path that he had followed and then down river
from his current resting spot. The water settled into a tranquil flow only
a few hundred feet ahead. There on the shore he spotted Sara's bright
red pack, and her body, lying motionless on the ground.

After surveying his position carefully, he realized that the narrow tree
branch he was balanced on could not be used to get to shore. It jutted
out from between two massive boulders that created a smooth-faced
wall ten feet high. Even if he could get to his rock climbing equipment
without falling off of the branch, he would have to fight off his vertigo
to climb the rock face. And even he were successful at overcoming
Mother Nature and his own fears, he would still be on the wrong side of
the river. He released the branch and plunged into the river, letting it
carry him to the spot where Sara lay.

"Sara," he called as he climbed out of the water. "Sara, talk to me." He
threw off his pack and knelt over her. "Sara!" he called more loudly as he
released her pack and pulled it off of her. He rolled her motionless body
onto her back. She had a strong carotid pulse, but didn't seem to be
breathing. Supporting her neck, he pulled her carefully out of the shal-
lows at the water's edge and laid her on a flat grassy spot. He knelt over
her and positioned her head to begin CPR. As he bent toward her
mouth she threw her arms around him and pressed her lips up firmly
against his. Her lips were cold, but the passionate kiss sent a warm flush
through his body.

"Miss Parker," he objected half heartedly, "are you trying to get me
fired?"

She giggled coyly.

"You scared the hell out of me," he said as she pulled his body closer,
still in the embrace that neither of them really wanted to release.

"I'm not your student anymore, James, I graduated. Remember?"

"Sara," he said more calmly, as he regained his composure. "Now is not the time for this discussion. We've got to radio back to the others to let them know we're O.K.. Why didn't you call us?"

"I must have hit my head on a rock. I was out until I heard your voice."

Smithson walked up the bank to where he had thrown his pack, and flipped it over. He pulled out the radio.

"Smithson to base, Smithson to base. Come in. Over."

He looked back at Sara, still sitting on the bank, as he waited for the response. She shrugged her shoulders and looked down at the ground, her short straight auburn hair falling in front of her face.

"Smithson to base....Jason, do you hear me? Over."

"Yo, Professor! Jason and the Argonauts standing by. That was close, Professor. We were just getting ready to head back and…"

"Abandon us?" Sara shouted over Smithson's shoulder.

"Sara! You O.K.?" Jason called back. "Of course we wouldn't abandon you. The prof left strict instructions: fifteen minutes and then we head back for help if we don't hear from you. Right, Professor?"

"Of course, Jason. We don't have time for this now, kids," he said as he glanced back at Sara's disapproving frown. "We've got to find a way back."

For the first time, Smithson looked up to study his surroundings. He had been so focused on Sara that he hadn't noticed where he was. His jaw dropped in amazement as the realization hit him.

"Wow," Sara sighed as she too realized that they were in an immense cavern.

"Yeah," Smithson replied, "Wow. This place must be at least ten miles in diameter. I've never seen or even heard of anything like this."

The low-hanging mist overhead made it difficult to see how high the roof was, but they could see at least a quarter-mile up the walls. Overhead, through the mist there were occasional breaks, but no blue sky was visible. The cavern was lit by multiple angles of light jutting through crevices in the cavern walls and ceiling, enough light to allow the rich flora and fauna to thrive in this lush paradise. It was like the muted light of a thinly clouded day.

It was apparent to Smithson that this was a self-contained ecosystem, protected from the outside world for an undeterminable span of time. The river that emanated from the waterfall originated from the fresh snowfalls of winter that melted through the crevices in the mountains with each springtime thaw. It provided an ample supply of water, which, in combination with the enclosed cavern roof, created a rainforest-like environment. Sara and the professor could see at least three species of birds flying overhead from where they sat on the grassy shores of the river, and the vegetation was a botanist's dream. Smithson ached to explore and catalogue the flora and fauna, many of which he was sure did not exist outside of this protected oasis, but he knew that would have to wait. Safe exit and entry would have to be established before any exploration would be done.

"Professor," Jason called back. "What's going on? Can you still hear me? What's your situation? Can you get back to us?"

"No. Not the way we came in. Even if we could get up to the waterfall, which we can't, there would be no way to get through it in that direction. No, we've got to find another way out. Stand by, Argonauts."

Smithson studied the walls of the cavern in the mountainside that formed the barrier through which they had entered. Like most of this vast cavern, the light seemed to shine in from multiple angles through openings between adjacent mountainous masses. The opening closest to the waterfall was about a quarter of a mile to the right of it and at least a hundred feet higher than the opening from which they had entered.

"Jason, listen closely."

Smithson described the location of this opening, and advised his students to head back to base camp. From there, they were to make contact with the authorities and organize a rescue party to try and locate the opening from the other side of the mountain. Fortunately, there was no snow at this low elevation in the summer, but it would still be a challenge. The rescue party would not have the advantage of a bright light pointing the way as Sara and the professor had from their vantage point inside the cavern. Although the cavern was well lit, the brightness was still quite muted compared to the outside sunlight.

Sara nimbly hoisted her pack and adjusted the straps after deflating the air bladders. "Ready when you are, James."

Smithson was uncomfortable with her new tone of familiarity. "Sara, please. That never happened. It was a moment of weakness."

"No, James. It's something that I've wanted to make happen for the longest time. It wasn't just plants that I came here to explore." She laughed and looked playfully in his direction. Although he was blushing, the look on his face told Sara that this was not the time. She cleared her throat, beginning to feel the warmth of a blush creeping up from her own neck. "Sorry, Professor. I'm ready."

Smithson secured the radio, careful to leave it active to receive, and donned his pack. "Let's go, then. The climb up to that opening is going to be a lot steeper than it looks from here. We'll be lucky to get up there by nightfall."

The river was bordered by a soft grassy bank that gave way to mossy underbrush as the light disappeared in the thick bed of ferns that lay under the evergreen canopy. They made their way along the riverbank to avoid having to cut through the thick forest. After about an hour of hiking along a gentle incline toward the canyon wall, the terrain changed dramatically. The vegetation thinned into a sparse outcropping of plants jutting through the rocky floor that led to the canyon wall. It was a strange sight. Smithson had approached many mountains in his day, but never one like this. Standing at the foothills of a vast mountain, watching it angle up toward the heavens is a sight never forgotten once experienced. It is a silent awe that has inspired many a poet over the centuries. But this mountain did not instill a sense of freedom, of vastness. Instead it created a stifling feeling of confinement. The closer they approached, the more the mountain seemed to arch up over their heads. They both began to wonder how they would ascend to the meeting point were they had hoped to exit, but as they closed in on the boundary, they noticed a series of hills counter-angled toward the mountainside and creating a path up toward their destination.

Smithson was uncomfortable with Sara's advances. She had stirred mixed emotions in him. Everything about her felt comfortable and exciting at the same time, but even though she had technically graduated, she was still here as his student. He hardly looked at her as he single-mindedly strode forward in search of the cavern exit.

"Hold up, Professor, I've got to rest a minute." Sara wasn't hurt by Smithson's rejection. She understood. She could see right through him and knew that he felt the same way about her as she felt about him; that it was just a matter of time. She also knew that this was not that time.

"Maybe you're right, Sara. We do need to reach the exit before it gets dark, but it's still early and once we start up, there may not be a place to rest. Look."

The foothills in front of them were a series of small peaks and ruts. The ruts were filled with loose small-to-medium-sized rocks that would surely make for poor footing. The intervening small peaks were smooth rock faces moist with dew from the overhanging fog. They would have to choose their path carefully.

Neither of them felt the need to force conversation, and after taking a drink and refilling their canteens, they awkwardly nodded to each other and resumed their trek. The footing was difficult, as expected. They slowly picked their way up through the foothills. Smithson led the way, looking back frequently to make sure Sara was able to maneuver safely. After about two hours of tediously slow hiking, they came to a small bluff at the crest of a hill. It was a flat area, which would provide a much-needed resting spot. The left side of the bluff abutted the side of the mountain, across from the drop-off to the cavern below, and at the far end it led to a narrow trail that wound its way up along the mountainside for another hundred yards or so, up to the window of light that Smithson had spotted from below. For the first time since they started toward it, he could see that it was indeed reachable by foot, but would be difficult. The trail was only about a yard wide and dropped off to the right, straight down toward the cavern bottom. He began to feel a sense of panic; just the sight of this obstacle unearthed from his memory the helpless feeling that his attacks of vertigo had brought on. One glance down at the wrong time could initiate a cascade in his nervous system that was certain to end in that disabling feeling, one that could be truly understood only by someone who had experienced vertigo. He felt the sweat beading up on his forehead, as he heard the scream.

Sara fell backward as she lost her footing on the loose rock just behind Smithson. He turned and lunged to grab her, and at that moment he too lost his footing and tumbled down toward her. Sara landed face up on a plateau and Smithson rolled helplessly on top of her, landing face to face. They looked at each other and burst out laughing.

"Heck of a way to break the ice," he said breathlessly.

"Not that I'm not enjoying this, James, but with that pack on your back and this rock bed I'm on, you're a bit heavy."

"Sorry," he said as he rolled to the side and scrambled to his feet. He held his hand down to help her up. "We'd better keep moving while we've got daylight."

"Thanks, prof," she said as he hoisted her to her feet.

They made their way carefully back up to the bluff. It was a level area about twenty feet wide and sixty feet long. As Smithson studied the terrain of the narrow trail at the far end of the bluff, Sara unshouldered her pack and leaned it against the rock wall to the left. She wandered over toward the right, where the edge of the bluff hung out over the lush valley far below. Off in the distance, Sara noticed a patchwork break in the trees and several small flumes of smoke rising up from the area. "James," she called, starting to feel more comfortable with the familiarity that circumstances had forced upon them. "What do you make of that?" she asked pointing toward the valley.

Smithson glanced over. "This valley must be inhabited, Sara; maybe a recreational campground." He took his pack off also, and pulled out his binoculars. He focused them toward the area the smoke was coming from and began to scan the terrain. "My God."

"What is it, James?"

There was no answer as Professor Smithson remained frozen, obviously mesmerized by what he saw.

"James!" she repeated, tugging at his shirt.

"Sorry, Sara," he replied as he reluctantly lowered his binoculars. "Here," he said as he handed them to her. "Take a look for yourself."

"I've never seen any cabins like those before. It's like a one-story apartment building made of logs. It's interesting, but I don't see what..."

"Scan to the left of there," Smithson interrupted. "About a hundred yards."

Sara slowly moved her head to the left, then froze as her jaw dropped wide open.

"Good Lord," she gasped, "what *are* they?"

"Hmmph. Good question. Do you see how their bodies are shaped?"

"Yeah," she said still fixated on her target through the binoculars. "Long arms and broad chins. And the ones wearing shorts...their legs are as thick as tree trunks. These guys would make a heck of defensive line."

"Yeah, but I don't think they'd be allowed to play."

"I don't know, James, I've seen some pretty strange ones on the football field."

"True, but they're all humans."

Sara pulled away from the binoculars and looked over at Professor Smithson. He continued to stare out into the jungle, even though he could see little more than vague clearings between the trees without the binoculars. "Unless I miss my guess, I'd say those people are descendants of the Neanderthals."

"They may be a little funny looking," she said, "but they sure look a lot more like us than like Neanderthals."

"You're fixed in time Sara. Remember, *Homo sapiens sapiens* have also changed a bit over the past forty thousand years. The people you're looking at are the evolved descendants of the Neanderthals."

"Parallel evolution."

Smithson nodded. "You've got it. They were never extinct, they just found a safe haven from our predecessors. They've probably evolved in this huge canyon for millennia. They may not even be aware of the outside world...of us."

"But wouldn't their curiosity have led them to explore? It's human nature to thirst for knowledge."

"True. But *they* are not human."

"Hey! Maybe they know a way out of here. Maybe they can help us."

"Maybe. But we can't make first contact without backup. If they do know about the outside world, they obviously don't want us to know about them. Our first priority has got to be to get the word out to the others."

"Agreed," Sara said.

The hike had been slow and it was late afternoon now. The light of the cavern was beginning to dim as the sun crept down the west side of the slopes outside. As it edged lower, the sun's direct rays broke through the opening for which they were headed and marked their destination like a laser pointer.

They studied the next part of the trail together. They appeared to be only about a hundred yards or so from the opening now. Although the light was beginning to dim, visibility in the cavern was still good.

"We'll never make it with these packs, James."

"Agreed. Take your radio, flashlight and food pack."

They stuffed their supplies into small fanny packs and buckled them on. Sara finished first, and darted out ahead. "See if you can keep up with me, prof!" she shouted playfully.

"Take it slow, Sara. We've got plenty of time and the footing doesn't look too good."

They headed off along the trail, which narrowed to two to three feet in parts and dropped off sharply into the forest bed below. They made their way sideways, leaning into the rock wall in front of them for balance. The tension grew as the path narrowed, and neither of them said a word. It took their full concentration to balance on the rocky trail. After a half hour of side-sliding along the path, Professor Smithson looked up to check their progress. As he turned his head toward the opening, the sickening feeling of vertigo began to overtake him.

"No!" he snapped, trying to break the spell before it accelerated. He focused his vision toward the rock wall in front of his face, hoping the stable surface would steady him, but it was hopeless. Once these spells started, they had to run their course.

Sara looked back as she heard him shout. "What is it? You scared the hell out of me."

Smithson didn't say a word, immersed in the concentration of trying to keep his balance. He could feel the control slipping away as his knees began to buckle. He put his right foot back and it landed on loose gravel at the path's edge. His body went limp as he slid helplessly off of the path.

"James!" Sara screamed. She was only about two yards in front of him on the path, but the drop-off was so steep she couldn't tell if he was clinging on. "James!"

"I'm O.K., Sara," she heard faintly.

Sara lay down on her stomach and looked over the ledge. Smithson was clinging to a small tree that was growing out of the rocks, his body hanging precariously out above the forest below.

"I'd hardly call that O.K.," she cried.

"It was the vertigo, Sara, but it's passed now. I guess I shocked it out of my system," he laughed.

They both heard a cracking noise and looked on in horror as the thin trunk of the tree began to break. Sara reached out and grabbed the trunk. "Hang on, James! Can you reach my hand?"

He held firmly to the branch. "Sara. Listen carefully. One of us has to make it out of here. This discovery is too important. If you hold on to that tree it'll pull us both down when it breaks. You've got to let go."

She bit back the tears, and gripped more tightly in determination. "Forget it! I've waited too long to be with you. I'm not going to lose you now."

He could feel his grip loosening. "Sara, if we both fall it's not going to help me. My best chance is if you can reach help." His left hand slipped from the branch and his body swung precariously over the canyon.

"No!" Sara screamed. "Grab my hand," she begged.

He looked up at her. "Sara, you've got to let go."

"No, James, I can't! I'll pull you up."

"You can't, Sara. I'm too heavy and you have no leverage."

The trunk cracked again, this time pulling Sara's body closer to the edge.

"I do love you, Sara," he said as he let go of the tree trunk.

"No!" she screamed as his body plunged through the canopy of tree-tops and out of sight into the underlying jungle. She called his name repeatedly, but there was no reply. She felt numb.

Sara lay motionless for several minutes, the tree trunk in her hand and the image of Smithson dropping silently into the forest below frozen into her mind. The pain of the gravel against her bare legs slowly began to reawaken her senses. She carefully pulled herself up to a sitting position, now becoming aware of her own precarious position. She had been so focused on Smithson's tragedy, that she had forgotten how tenuous her own situation was. She leaned back against the wall.

"Think, Sara. Think," she said aloud as she fought to regain her composure. "Of course, the radio!" She dug into her fanny pack and pulled out the radio. They had decided to keep only one radio on standby at a time to monitor for the others, in order to preserve their batteries. It was Smithson's radio that was set to standby when he fell.

She clicked her radio on. "James! James, can you hear me?"

She listened carefully. She was sure she heard a faint break in the background static, but it didn't repeat. She called out again, and listened hopefully. Several times she thought she may have heard a change in the background noise that could have been the professor, and tried repeatedly to answer it. After several moments she began to come to the realization that there was no answer, that her mind was creating what it so badly wanted to hear.

Sara became aware of the dimming light. Her chances of making it to the opening before darkness enveloped the cavern would fade with the light, and she knew that she would not likely survive a night on this ledge. She carefully placed the radio back in her pack, leaving it on standby, and pulled herself to her feet. She leaned gently into the rock wall and resumed her slow ascent. The opening to the outside world glowed orange with the light of the setting sun, and the cavern darkened behind her as she entered the small cave.

It was shaped like a tube of granite about fifteen feet in diameter and twenty feet long. It was cool inside and the enclosure instilled a welcomed sense of security in Sara after the treacherous path she had been negotiating for the past two hours. A small stream of fresh water flowed slowly through from the outside mountains, creating a peaceful trickling sound. Sara's muscles relaxed, and as the tension crept out of her body a sense of exhaustion overtook her. She knelt down to the stream and rinsed herself with the cool refreshing water. It was much more appealing than the now-warm water in her canteen, and she poured out the stale water and refilled her canteen with the fresh water, stopping frequently to quench her thirst. Refreshed but still tired, she found a dry niche in the cave and settled down. It was too dark to look outside and see if the rescue party was nearby. Sara pulled the radio out of her pack and tried to raise Jason, but there was no answer. She longingly tried a few more times to contact the professor as well. This time her mind did not create the illusion of hope. She was beginning to accept the likely fate of her new love. She was too tired to eat and drifted off to sleep with the radio at her side, and the image of James Smithson frozen in time and space above the canopy of trees, his voice trailing off to an ethereal whisper as he said, "I do love you, Sara." She smiled sadly as she slipped into a much-needed deep sleep.

*   *   *   *   *   *   *   *

"Do...read m...? Answer me if.... can....me. We can't..... opening...think we're near...said it.....be." The soft soothing sound of trickling water was joined by the intermittent crackling of the radio, and melded with Sara's dreams. Half asleep, she smiled as she dreamt of Jason coming through the cave to find her.

"Sara? Professor? Can you hear me? Over." It was coming through more clearly now, and Sara's eyes began to open as she emerged from her dream state. She squinted as the light of day met her half-open eyes. "Sara? Professor Smithson? Do you read me? Answer me if you can hear me. We can't see the cave opening, but we think we're near the spot where you said it would be."

"My God!" Sara was wide awake now. "They found me."

She quickly grabbed for the radio and knocked it off of its base, sending it tumbling down into the running stream below. "Damn it!" She lunged down and pulled it out of the water. "Jason! I'm here," she shouted, pressing the send button. "You found me."

Sara listened intently for the reply, but none came. "Jason! Can you hear me?" She desperately called into the damp walky-talky. Still there was no reply.

"Son of a bitch!" she blurted out.

Sara made her way to the cave exit, but couldn't get close enough to see anything without risking losing her footing and plunging out into unknown terrain. She called again, but the radio was still dead.

"Sara, you jerk," she said, smacking her forehead as she realized the water must have damaged the radio. She opened the battery compartment, dried the contacts with her tee shirt, then slipped the battery pack back into place and flipped the switch on.

"…. we're going to move on," came Jason's voice.

"No!" she shouted. She hit the send button again. "Jason, don't go. I'm right here. Can you hear me?"

"Sara!" came a reply. "Sara, is that you?"

"No. It's the Queen of England, you jerk! Of course it's me. Get up here and save my butt."

The search party was able to hone in on her radio signal and triangulate a location. The rescue was difficult, but they were able to get Sara out that day. The opening was on a sheer face of the mountainside, and they had to airlift her out. A search team was airlifted in the next day, led by Sara. There was an exhaustive search, but no sign of Professor Smithson could be found. They couldn't find his radio signal or his body, which the searchers assumed must have been pulled away to the lair of some local wildlife for food.

Although no one believed her story at first, the search party returned with pictures of the creatures that inhabited the cavern. The pictures were digitally enhanced, and studied by the leading anthropologists in the area. The consensus was that these indeed *could* be descendants of Neanderthal man, and interest around the world was piqued by the intrigue and implications of this discovery. Money to fund a formal expedition flowed in. By the time the politics of the situation could be worked out, nearly a month had passed before the expedition was ready to enter. A series of stairs and platforms had been built into the side of the mountain to reach the small cave opening a quarter of a mile up the side of the mountain.

CHAPTER XVII

First Contact

Scientists and politicians, religious leaders and entrepreneurs all debated about who should make first contact, and how it should be done. In the end, a team composed of anthropologists, linguists, photographers, journalists, diplomats, engineers, a physician and a sizable military force was assembled. Although hotly contested, the presence of the relentless Sara Parker was eventually allowed.

Exactly five weeks to the day after Sara's fateful slip into the waterfall, the expedition of thirty men and women reentered the cavern from the small opening through which Sara had escaped. The heavy equipment was encased in watertight crates and thrust into the waterfall. The team gathered the equipment as it floated downstream to the spot where Sara had first landed on shore. It was from this point that the exploration would begin.

The details of first contact largely depended on which member of the expedition told the story, but the original digital video disc on which the events were recorded by the team's journalists clearly shows Sara out in front of the group as they approached a lone Neanderthal farming the fields outside the housing development. His initial territorial defense reaction also demonstrated just how quickly Sara could run as she darted behind the soldiers for protection. A fierce roar of rage and the body language of the Neanderthal facing a score of weapons pointed at him confirmed that he had not had contact with armed men before. Fortunately, calmer heads prevailed. The linguists and diplomats proved useful as the Neanders turned out to be a very peaceful race in spite of their fearsome appearance.

Weapons were lowered, and the Neander began to drop his guard. As the first man approached him alone, the farmer looked him in the eye and said, "James."

"What?" Sara called out. "Did he say James?" she asked as she darted forward through the line of soldiers.

The Neander looked at her strangely. She was the only woman on the expedition other than the physician and linguist who he had not yet spotted.

"Did you say James?" she asked him.

"James," he repeated, this time pointing back toward the village.

"My God," she said. "They found him. Is he all right?" she asked. "Is James all right?"

The Neander looked puzzled. "James," he repeated again motioning to the village.

The linguist stepped forward. "He obviously doesn't understand you, but there must be someone back at the village named James who he wants us to see. Judging from their language pattern it's unlikely that's a name native to their language. It's got to be another human who wandered in here. I'd say there's a good chance that he found Professor Smithson, and if he did, the professor must have still been alive at the time. That's the only way this Neanderthal would could know how to say James."

The farmer led them to an outpost outside the village, manned by four Neanders, all similarly dressed. He spoke to them briefly, as the linguist listened, fascinated.

"What did they say?" inquired the expedition commander.

"I've no idea. I've never heard a language pattern like that before."

The group settled in. Within a half hour, a large group of Neanders returned. The one in front was dressed quite differently from the others, more formally. Around him was a large group of stout Neander men, all in some sort of uniform and bearing weapons the likes of which the commander had never seen.

"What are we up against?" he asked his technical advisor.

"The unknown, sir," was his only reply.

Neither side was anxious to move against the unknown strength of the other.

A moment later, four Neanders broke through ranks to the front, carrying a stretcher. A head popped up from the stretcher and perused the group.

"Sara! Thank God you're all right."

Sara and James Smithson would largely be credited with the discovery of the modern day Neanderthals.

CHAPTER XVIII

The Seeds of Discontent

First contact was awkward, but the linguists were finally able to establish communication, and a study of Neander society ensued. They were a surprisingly intelligent species, with unparalleled technical skills and a masterful capability for mimicry. They had developed basic tools for agriculture and construction, but there was an obvious absence of technology for such skillful artisans. Much like the American Indians, they had learned to live as a part of their environment, in harmony with nature. They were therefore able to maintain the balance of their ecosystem. However, unlike the native Americans, they homesteaded in one place. They had no interest in exploration. In fact, this proved to be the primary social difference between the Neanderthals and the *Homo sapiens* who had evolved into modern day humans. The Neanders lacked the basic instinct to explore, to discover not only new places, but also new technology. This lack of desire for change and discovery prevented the natural evolution that would have ensued if they had been human, the development that would have surely overwhelmed and destroyed this sheltered microcosm. Their technological ignorance had insured their preservation. They had evolved perfectly for their environment. First contact would change that forever.

Once exposed to the influence of humankind, the Neanders' innate drive to mimic the technology, food, language and culture they were exposed to took control of their destiny. Over the ensuing three generations they were mainstreamed into human society. Their homeland, over the fierce protestation of the Smithsons, would become a destination tourist attraction. This assured the destruction of a once-perfect ecosystem. There was no turning back.

By the mid-twenty-first century, the Neanders were a part of Earth culture. They intermingled with humans in most walks of society, excelling of course in technical jobs, and were banned from sports in which their physical prowess would prove a danger to their more frail human counterparts. As they settled into various communities, the inevitable seeds of human prejudice were planted around Earth, as they had been each time throughout human history that a group possessing traits different from those of the status quo was introduced into the homogeneousness of a society. The new group would be an agitating force, invariably viewed as inferior until they too would melt into the oneness of society, diluting the very diversity that makes a society strong. The seeds of discontent were sewn with each Neanderthal family that relocated to a new community, taking human jobs and interacting with human families. And the seeds grew like weeds in freshly spread mulch. They could not be controlled without being destroyed.

As the Neanders mainstreamed into human society, resentment grew geometrically. There was tremendous resentment of the new members of society who were eager, hardworking, and content to excel at their jobs without any desire to advance up the corporate or political ladders. The frequency of confrontations grew as the Neanders increased in numbers and their presence throughout society expanded. Though normally not confrontational, they never hesitated to defend themselves or their families. Any attack against a Neanderthal by a human would inevitably result in human injury at the hands of the powerful Neanders. This only served to further inflame the tensions.

By the twenty-second century, the Neanderthals were nearly one hundred thousand strong. They proved to be very hardy creatures, but because of their obvious evolutionary differences they were never able to truly assimilate into the society that had melted away a multitude of human cultures in the past. In spite of their determined efforts to meld into society, the increasing violence, which reached a level only definable as terrorism, made even governmental intervention futile. The Neanders began to form their own cities and their own society within society, but would never be more than second-class citizens on Planet Earth.

CHAPTER XIX

Teconea

The twenty-second century saw what was probably the greatest techno-logical advance in human history, the light-speed space-drive system. It was termed warp drive, in part because of the physics behind the engine, and in part because this was already so established among sci-ence fiction fans of the nineteenth and twentieth centuries that it had found its way into the pages of Webster's Dictionary. This system revo-lutionized space exploration and, for the first time, made off-Earth col-onization practical. This was long considered critical to the survival of the human species, particularly as scientists uncovered evidence that not only the dinosaurs, but also several other advanced life forms had been destroyed by cataclysmic events on Earth over the millennia. Although many humans were anxious to blame these events on alien civilizations, meteors were considered the most likely culprits. In either case, it became clear that humankind would be the next dominant life form to become extinct if a way off of the planet were not found.

Warp drive had solved this dilemma. The failure of the attempted settlement of the Orion system in the twenty-second century led to the development of a more extensive deep-space probe program. For many years, the program was fruitless due to the very limited speed of pre-warp space travel; however, with the development of a rudimentary warp drive system the program became viable. The earliest warp drive systems were used only on unmanned probes, but greatly expedited the exploration of deep space. By the early twenty-third century, a suitable planet had been located approximately twenty-two light years from Earth and was designated planet Alpha One. Soon after this discovery, manned ships had been fitted with warp drive systems in hopes of deep space exploration and colonization. Unfortunately, the early warp drive systems were relatively slow; calculations indicated it would take eight years to reach Alpha One. Few volunteers were willing to donate nearly half their lives to space travel and settlement of an unknown destination. The plight of the Neanders became the obvious solution to the problem. By this point in history, they were anxious to once again find relief from the aggressive *Homo sapiens*. In addition to their desire for a home without human interference, their strong physical makeup and superb technical skills made them ideal candidates for the arduous trip.

The first ship reached Alpha One in 2225, bearing a team of forty-eight men and women—all Neanderthal descendants. The planet was found to be more Earth-like than expected. Although temperatures were less than hospitable on the planet as a whole, its equatorial region proved to be quite pleasant and rich in natural resources. Polar ice caps covered nearly a third of the planet's surface, but along the equator, temperatures ranged around 70 degrees Fahrenheit throughout the year. Life forms consisted of a variety of flora and fauna, but no intellectually-advanced life forms were detected in the settlers' surveys. The planet seemed perfect.

During the twenty years that it took for the first settlers to arrive, establish a colony and complete their planetary survey, space travel technology had continued to advance on Earth. Hyperspatial travel had been greatly advanced, and a large transport vessel capable of carrying twenty-five hundred people was built to speed the settlement of Alpha One. The trip had been reduced to a six-month journey by the time this ship had been completed, and the appeal of exploration increased exponentially with the lure of minimum time lost in transit. The first ship carried a variety of workers from all walks of life. They were primarily the Neanders who were anxious to escape persecution on Earth, but about one hundred humans also made the trip.

The success of the colonization far exceeded even the most optimistic expectations. Within forty years of the first landing there was a thriving colony, composed not only of military explorers and scientists, but of civilians representing all professions. In 2265, with no remaining doubt that this was the first successful colonization of another planet by Earth's inhabitants, Alpha One was renamed The Earth Colony ONE Alpha, or TECONEA. The acronym was later dropped in favor of the name Teconea.

Development of Teconea proceeded with amazing speed. More in-depth surveys had uncovered an abundance of geological materials that were in sparse supply on Earth. The allure of vast diamond mines and a source of titanium far greater than any previously located rapidly accelerated the colonization of the planet. The additional discovery of nutonium by some of the human scientists provided the previously-missing source of energy needed to advance transwarp travel to a more practical level. Nutonium powered vehicles needed to carry only a fraction of the fuel supply their predecessors had required, and achieved speeds many times that of the earliest warp drive systems. Even large colonization vessels could make the trip from Earth to Teconea in less than a week by the late twenty-third century.

By the turn of the millennium, all the Neanders had been resettled to Teconea. The Teconeans flourished on their new planet, and by the mid-twenty-fourth century were four million strong. With the separation of time and space, the two worlds developed increasingly different cultures. As they continued to grow apart, their mistrust for one another also grew, and other than for the trade vessels that were a necessity for both worlds, there was very little direct contact between the two species. With the exception of diplomatic envoys and starship trade crews, there were no humans on Teconea by the mid-twenty-fourth century.

The twenty-fourth century also saw the first rapid development of outworlds for both Teconea and Earth. The advent of transwarp drive by humans and the efficient and prolific mining of nutonium by the Teconeans provided the first economically-feasible solution for developing inhabitable planets that were light years away from their home worlds. Because there were far more humans on Earth than there were Neanderthals on Teconea, human colonies developed more rapidly. However, the competitive nature of the Teconeans narrowed the gap in numbers as the decades passed. The average Teconean family had six children, encouraged by their government to multiply as quickly as possible. The rapidly-increasing Teconean population, combined with the vast wealth which their home world provided and their innate technological skills, allowed them to develop a vast fleet of settlement ships, as well as an ever-more-formidable armada of military vessels.

The settlement of multiple outworlds by human colonists proceeded at a steady pace throughout the twenty-fourth century, and by the turn of the twenty-fifth century, there were a dozen planets with thriving new human civilizations. The population of each planet swelled as travel became less expensive and many of the twenty billion inhabitants of Earth sought refuge on pristine worlds that offered new hope and adventure. They were lands of opportunity, much as the western frontier had seemed to Americans in the 1800's. The new planets attracted the more adventurous risk-takers, and each planet cultivated its own personality as populations swelled with new generations who had never known life on Earth. Each, however, shared a common fear of the Teconeans who were growing ever more aggressive and distant from the Earth culture from which they were born.

The Teconeans had been developing in a similar pattern throughout the twenty-fourth century, but at a slower pace. This was in part due to their smaller numbers, but was also caused by their technological inferiority. Although they were masterful at reproducing high quality products, they lacked the spirit of innovation their human counterparts possessed, and were forced to rely on their ability to duplicate human technology to advance. Much of this technology could be acquired through trade; a necessity for the humans who needed the cheap and extensive supply of nutonium available on Teconea. However, as tensions between the two civilizations grew, military advances on Earth were protected from the Teconeans with ever-increasing levels of security. These secrets could be obtained only through espionage. Although the Teconeans' appearance hindered them from infiltrating human technocenters, their ability to offer great wealth to interested parties provided them with an ample supply of human spies to keep their military up to date and only one close step behind their enemies on Earth.

The increasing threat of Teconean aggression forced the cohesiveness that characterized the outworlds of human development. Although each world had its own personality and cherished its independence, they all required the protection of Earth's powerful military Space Corps. The alliance was formalized as the United Federation of Planets in 2403, and the acceptance of Earth's Omnicenter and Space Corps were adopted as the official political and military organizational centers for the Federation.

The Teconeans, though less structured and more contentious within their own ranks, were able to develop a united organization based on a common hatred of humanity, which grew through the years. Theirs was a military-social structure led by the Emperor of Teconea, and each of the seven Teconean outworlds was headed by a military governor who answered only to the Emperor. The Teconean Empire was driven by a single desire: to one day take back the home world from which they had come. They felt that Earth was their birthright, and that the humans who had banished them from it had to be annihilated in order for them to accomplish their goal.

The development of the Federation had evolved in a fan-like pattern, with Earth at its core and the outworlds dispersed in a semiglobal pattern away from Earth. The Teconean planets were arranged in a similar pattern nearly the mirror image of the Federation's. They were like two halves of a globe in space, each fanning out from Earth and Teconea at their centers, separated by a neutral zone where development was thwarted by the fear of proximity to the enemy.

By the mid-twenty-fifth century tensions were high, as the Teconean military had grown large enough to threaten the safety of the Federation. The Teconean Empire had amassed a vast fleet of attack ships, but lacked the structured command system necessary to coordinate such a massive war. Earth had had two centuries to fortify its defense systems, and would not be easily penetrated by conventional weapons. Federation intelligence had information that an attack was imminent, but its sources on Teconea were unable to locate a command technocenter or attack-fleet staging area capable of coordinating a successful large-scale attack against the Federation.

CHAPTER XX

Tri-Luna

The characteristic deep red glow blanketed the nighttime surface of Tri-Luna, a small planet located in the Orion system. It had been chosen as the military base for the growing Teconean forces and tactical coordination center for the Empire over two centuries after their banishment from Earth to the planet of Teconea. The deceptively beautiful planet possessed the rare quality of three moons, which traveled in a synchronous orbit around the planet, casting a ubiquitous glow of deep red light across most of the surface every night of the year, except during periods of heavy cloud cover. This ambient light allowed a twenty-four hour a day economy for the ambitious settlers, as well as a measure of security for the Teconean warriors who instinctively watched their backs at every turn. In addition, the heavy ion storms of the outer belt of the Orion solar system provided cover from the deep space long-range scanners deployed by the Federation. The area had been ignored by the Federation since the failed attempt to settle the planet in the twenty-second century. The hardy Teconeans had been much more successful at adapting to the cold temperatures and 1.2 g's of gravitational pull than their human counterparts had been three centuries earlier. The Teconeans had used the supplies abandoned by the failed settlement party from Earth to establish a new colony, then had developed the area as an attack base. Its proximity to Earth, combined with the natural protection of the ion storms of Orion, made it a perfect choice. It had remained a complete secret to the Federation until a small trade ship captained by Danny Stryker had stumbled upon it while returning from a viridium ore pick-up on Teconea in 2497.

Stryker and his copilot T.C. McGee carried only consumer goods on their trade routes, mostly precious gems or industrial materials of no military significance, but a search and seizure by military patrols intent on uncovering technospies was an annoyance to be avoided. Stryker was also anxious to deliver his shipment and get to Omnicenter as quickly as possible to discover why, after so many years of civilian life, his old commander, Alexander Thompson was summoning him back to Space Corps Command. The ion storms of Orion provided convenient cover for a trade vessel trying to avoid military police or space pirates, but only an experienced starship pilot like Stryker would be bold enough to pilot manually through the ion storms that made navigation computers useless. It was for this reason that he often marked his routes to pass close to Orion. The camouflage provided by ion storms had saved him more than once, but he'd never been fired on by a Teconean battle cruiser before. His close encounter with Teconean forces in the Orion system was the first clue the Federation would have as to the location of the Teconean military technocenter.

*   *   *   *   *   *   *   *

The main spaceport of the Tri-Luna militia headquarters was located about ten miles outside the capital city. Beck could see the sun setting over the stark skyline of the austerely-built business district in the background, as the red hue of night began to envelop the heavily-fortressed spaceport where he was requesting clearance to land. Even Stryker and McGee had to admire the rare beauty created by the light of the setting sun reflecting off of the three moons of Tri-Luna, a sight visible only from a trajectory like the one the Stargazer was using to approach the Teconean spaceport. But the two men knew well that this exquisite beauty masked the true nature of the planet below.

The ship landed in a heavily guarded bay. By the time the ship had been secured by Teconean forces, T.C. had regained control of his legs. Beck had placed the EM-pulse weapon on a low setting, and the damage inflicted on T.C. and Danny Stryker had only been temporary. Shortly after the ship docked, the Stargazer was boarded by four Teconean security guards. Trailing closely behind and hidden from Stryker's view by the large Teconean warriors was a petite woman in civilian clothes. She walked over to Beck and threw her arms around him.

"Hans, I was so worried. Thank God you're all right. Did you get it?"

Danny spun in his chair and looked up in horror as he heard the voice. "Jen?"

Beck burst out laughing. "Again you lose, hero."

Danny and T.C.'s eyes were fixed on Dr. Jennifer Lee.

"Why, Jen?" was all Danny could say, the pain echoing in his voice.

She looked away without saying a word.

"I've got it!" Beck exclaimed as he looked back at Jennifer. "It's in Stryker's saddlebag. It's back in his quarters. Watch them," he said to the guards. "I'll get the obelisk."

"No, Hans. You take care of things here. I'll get it." She turned and walked back to the ship's quarters.

Beck turned back to Danny with a smug look of victory on his face. "Why?" he sniped. "It's quite obvious, really. I'm surprised that a trader like you, a businessman, would have to ask. Jennifer and I have worked diligently for years, devoting our lives to Omnicenter, and have never reaped a unit of profit from our discoveries. We live like drone workers on a planet infested with drone workers. Our lives were meaningless. The wealth of the Empire was at our feet for merely passing our inventions in their direction. The FDS was the coupe de grace that has insured us endless wealth. We have built a duplicate FDS array here on Tri-Luna, and only have to activate it with the obelisk in order to realize our dream."

"And live under Teconean rule as a subordinate human? Some great business deal, Beck. You may be a marshmallow, but Jen isn't that stupid."

"My foolish friend," Beck laughed again. "The Teconeans have no need of the Federation. They only want to reclaim the Earth from which they came. They have as much right to it as we humans. The outworlds are of no interest to the Empire, and Jennifer and I will have our pick of them. We can live like royalty on any of the outworlds with the wealth we've earned from our neighbors."

"And the inhabitants of Earth?" Danny asked, shaking his head.

"A small price to pay. The Empire will resettle them on outworlds. They will be thankful in the long run, having been freed from that overcrowded rock and their mundane existence toiling under a rigid Federation government. Humanity will be reborn."

"You fool" T.C. muttered. "Do you really think they'll settle for that? Do you think they want a peaceful coexistence with us; that they won't crush us out of existence once given half a chance?"

Jennifer emerged from the crew's quarters, triumphantly holding the obelisk above her head. "It's beautiful! The key to our future." She walked over to Beck and threw her left arm around him, cradling the obelisk in her right as she planted a kiss firmly on his lips.

Hans Beck smiled wryly as he motioned to the guards to take the prisoners away. One of the large Teconean warriors walked over to the two men still restrained in their fused safety harnesses. He withdrew a small saber from his belt, and with great alacrity that stemmed from his military training, cut the men loose, each with a single stroke. He ordered them out of their seats, with saber still in hand. They responded slowly, stiff from the confines of their recent flight. Danny was still nursing his sore arm, which was just beginning to respond to his attempts to move it as the EM-pulse damage was wearing off.

"Help your friend," Beck barked at him as T.C. struggled to stay on his feet, still wobbly from the shock to his spinal cord.

Danny glared at Beck as he put his good arm around T.C.'s waist and helped him out the door, escorted by the four guards. He stopped at the outer hatch and glanced back to see Jennifer still resting in Beck's arms, a tranquil smile on her face, and then turned away.

"Let's get out of here."

The guards led their prisoners through the space dock and headed for the security bays. It was a dark and dreary building compared to the one at Space Corps Command. The warriors of Teconea shunned the niceties of life; they felt luxury would make them soft. Although the civilian buildings on the home world of Teconea were similarly appointed to those on Earth, Tri-Luna was different. This was a military base. Its buildings were functional but nothing more. A minimum of power was expended on light and climate control, and the decor was a uniform dull gray metallic finish. The long corridor from the spaceport dock to the adjacent military command center was cold and sparsely inhabited. Their footsteps echoed monotonously as they proceeded without a word passing among the six men.

Danny and T.C. walked down the long, dark corridor flanked by the four Teconean warriors. They found themselves breathing rapidly as they labored against Tri-Luna's 1.2 g's of gravitational pull. As they neared the end of the corridor, they approached a massive steel portal. One of the warriors entered a code in a glowing access panel at the left of the doorway and the large steel doors slowly slid open, revealing a vestibule with a transparent doorway at the far end. The guard stepped in and motioned the others to follow. Danny hesitated for a few seconds and felt a firm nudge from behind. He glanced back, ready to protest, but saw the look on the face of the Teconean warrior and decided against it.

They proceeded into the vestibule and the steel doors shut tightly behind them. Through the transparent door in front of them, they could see a large, round room about eighty yards across, bustling with activity. This room was lit much more brightly than the corridor they had just left. The room's ambient light settings were more like what they were accustomed to on human planets. From this chamber, several corridors led off in different directions like the spokes of a wheel, and the glass entrance was heavily guarded. This was obviously the entrance from the military spaceport into the command center of Tri-Luna.

Once they were all in the small entry vestibule with the steel doors shut behind them, a Teconean guard in a drab gray uniform approached the doorway and began to question the warrior who had led the group in about the nature of their visit. He explained that Danny and T.C. were prisoners being transferred to the detention block for holding. The guard eyed the two men up and down. He grunted and waved the six of them through the glass doors and into the large hall.

Unlike the dark, deserted corridor that led them here, this chamber was bustling with activity, though no one seemed to be paying attention to anyone or anything except their own private destinations. Several of the Teconeans were armed warriors dressed in the same metallic-embossed uniforms as the four who had escorted Danny and T. C., but most wore the drab gray uniforms that the security guard had on. Other than a series of stripes on their shirt pockets, each uniform was identical. Danny surmised that the stripes were rank insignias. Those with more stripes seemed to strut with greater self-assurance, reinforcing his suspicions. None of them, however, seemed to have any emotion at all.

"What's happened to these people, Danny?" asked T.C..

"What do you mean?"

"From everything I've heard, from what we've seen on our trade routes, Neanders are a passionate people. That was part of the reason they could never assimilate into Earth culture."

"What, are you kidding, buddy? Look at these people. No matter what their personalities, they wouldn't have been accepted. Humans have never tolerated those who couldn't become like them. Not even among different races of humans. They never would have accepted Neanders."

T.C. shook his head. "You may be right, Danny, but still…"

"Yeah, I see what you mean. These Teconeans don't look like they have much passion for anything. They're drones."

"No fear," T.C. said numbly.

"They've turned their military into dispassionate warriors with no preference for life over death. The worst kind of enemy."

"Quiet, you two!" barked one of their escorts.

Danny turned to respond. Danny had a reputation for always getting in the last word. But once again, he saw the vicious glare on the face of the Teconean guard, and thought silence would be the better part of valor.

The guards led them down the second corridor to the right off of the central great hall, toward the detention cellblock. When they arrived, they were turned over to two of the gray uniformed Teconeans who were apparently the keepers of the sparsely populated prison. In fact, Danny noticed, he and T.C. were the only prisoners in the otherwise deserted security area. They were placed together in a single cell. It was a stark room with nothing but two thinly-padded slabs to lie on, and a small hygiene cubicle in the back. The two prison guards led them in without a word, then secured the door behind them and walked back around the corner to their office, out of sight of the prisoners.

Danny flopped down wearily on one of the slabs as T.C. stood by the door and watched their captors stride away indifferently. "Not too concerned about us, huh?"

"Would you be? It's not exactly like we blend in here. Where are we going to go even if we do figure a way out of this cell?"

T.C. looked out toward the cellblock entrance, then glanced back at Danny and shrugged his shoulders.

"I don't know about you, but I'm wiped," Danny said. "Might as well get some shut eye. It's their move next."

He lay back on the uncomfortable bunk and struggled to find a tolerable position. T.C. suddenly became aware of the strain that the gravity had on his body, still recovering from the temporary paralysis of the EM-pulse injury. He shrugged again and sat down on the vacant bunk. He looked over at Danny who was already fast asleep.

How does he do that? he thought. T.C. could never clear his mind that fast. It was just another of the things that amazed him about Danny Stryker, one of those things that set Danny apart, that allowed him to function just a little better than everyone else. T.C. lay back and stared at the ceiling. There was no point in closing his eyes; he would see too many things. It was better to just wait until they closed by themselves, which happened more rapidly than he had anticipated. T.C. was exhausted and sleep overtook him quickly in spite of the events of the day. Both of the men slept soundly in the silence of the cell.

T.C. stirred from his sleep, rubbing his dry eyes and adjusting to the light of the cell. He was momentarily disoriented as ethereal dreams seeped out of his mind and the starkness of the cell walls brought him back to reality. He turned toward Danny and saw the figure of Jennifer Lee leaning over Danny and reaching toward him.

"Hey! Get your hands off him."

Her head turned quickly toward T.C..

"Quiet," she whispered harshly. "We don't have much time."

"Time for what? Haven't you done enough damage already?"

Danny reached up and grabbed her arms, pulling them down behind her back with a firm grasp on her wrists.

"Ow! Danny, what are you doing? We don't have time for this."

Danny stood up behind her, tightening his grip. "What's the matter, sweetheart? Is Hans going to get jealous?"

"Don't be ridiculous. Couldn't you see through it? I must be a better actress than I thought," she said.

"Give me a break, Jen. I saw the look in your eyes when you fell into his arms."

"Look, loverboy, hold your pride in check for a minute. We've known for some time that the Teconeans were hiring Omnicenter personnel as moles to bring new technology to the Empire. As outstanding as they are as technicians, the Neanders have never had the aptitude to develop technology fast enough to keep up with the Federation. About two years ago, I began to suspect that Beck might be one of the moles. In fact, with his level of security clearance, he figured to be the key to the military technology leak that had been keeping the Teconean Empire in pace with the Federation. I began to nurture a relationship with him in hopes of winning his confidence. It didn't prove to be too hard to win the affection of that lonely, pathetic man. He was so desperate for companionship that he opened up to me like a letter waiting to be read."

"When he told me of his plans to sell the FDS to the Teconeans, he had such a smug smile on his face that I wanted to kill him on the spot. But I held my emotions in check long enough to discuss things with General Thompson. He convinced me that our best chance of stopping the Empire's plan was for me to stay close to Beck. After talking to Thompson, I realized that if I were to expose Beck, the Empire would just hire someone else and we would be back to square one. I've kept up the charade until now. If we don't do something quickly, they'll activate the FDS and that will spell the end of the Federation as we know it. We've got to act quickly."

"Did you sleep with him, Jen?"

"What!" she snapped. "The Federation is about to be destroyed, and all you can think about is your ego?"

Danny just stared at her.

"No! O.K.?" she said indignantly. "Now can we get on with this?"

Danny stood motionless, maintaining his grip tightly around her wrists. "How do we know we can trust you?"

"We don't," T.C. broke in, "but we don't have a lot of options here, Danny. Do you see another way out? I'm all ears if you've got a better plan."

"I guess you're right." Danny released his grip on Jennifer. "So what's your plan, Jen?"

"As I said, we don't have much time." She rubbed her aching wrists, glaring at Danny. "The FDS is too heavily guarded for us to recover the obelisk. The only chance we have of stopping them is to get to the Stargazer and try to torpedo it from the air."

She reached into a shoulder bag she carried and pulled out three metallic rings, each about a foot in diameter, with a small black tube on one side and a small red tube of equal proportions on the opppposite side.

"Here, put these on."

They each took a ring as she handed it to them, and studied it carefully, turning it slowly around in their hands in an attempt to figure out what it was.

Jennifer slipped the third ring over her head and twisted the small black tube in the front. The two men stared incredulously as Jennifer's appearance slowly began to change, starting at the ring around her neck, in both an upward and downward direction, transforming her appearance into that of a Teconean man. Her face was completed first, and Danny stepped back instinctively at the sudden proximity of a Teconean. Even her smell seemed to change. As he stepped back, he saw her shapely figure transform from the neck down into the squat powerful physique of a Neanderthal. All he could think of at that moment was that he had made love to this creature. His stomach turned.

Danny just stared in disgust, but T.C. reached out to touch the new stranger in front of him. His hand seemed to reach right through the Teconean's chest and came to rest on Jennifer's soft, supple breast.

"Heh! Watch what you're grabbing, big guy," Jennifer's voice rang out from the Teconean who stood in front of them. "It's a new holoemitter that Quigley's developed. Pretty cool, huh?"

"Incredible," he gasped.

"But obviously," she said, looking at T.C. as he quickly pulled his hand away from her breast, "don't let anyone or anything brush up against you or your cover will be blown."

The two men slipped the rings over their heads and twisted the black tubes. They watched each other's transformations in fascination. Once the change was complete, the three of them looked at each other and burst out laughing.

"One more thing," Jennifer said as she reached around to the back of the ring and twisted the small red tube, now obscured by the holoimage of the Teconean she appeared to be. "Don't forget to turn the red voice-control tube." The two men were startled as a deep guttural voice came out of Jennifer's new body. It was still in standard Federation English, but clearly Teconean in quality.

The two men twisted the red tubes and tested their voices.

"Ready?" rang out Jennifer's new voice.

"Let's do it."

The three of them headed out of the cell and past the bodies of the two guards Jennifer had stunned to gain entry into the cellblock. They pulled the bodies into a cell and out of sight, then took a deep breath and headed out into the main atrium that led back to the spaceport. Just before they entered the atrium, Jennifer turned toward the two men.

"You two stay behind me and let me do all of the talking. I'm more familiar with Teconean military protocol than you are, and we can't afford any mistakes. Here," she said reaching into her shoulder bag once more. "I've got one more goody in my bag of tricks."

Jennifer reached into her bag and handed each of them a compact hand phaser. "Careful how you use these things. They have a limited range and a short lasting energy supply. It keeps them nice and compact, easy to conceal. Unfortunately, though, they're not much of a match power-wise for a standard issue hand phaser or even a Teconean EM-pulse emitter, for that matter."

The three of them concealed their weapons carefully behind the broad belts of their holographic uniforms. Jennifer tossed her shoulder bag into a desk drawer, then turned back to the men. She led them into the main atrium, which still bustled with activity. Much as they expected, the Teconean workers ignored them, each heading his own way. They made a point of keeping their distance, nonetheless, and headed toward the security station that monitored the entrance to the spaceport. Jennifer, camouflaged in the uniform of a Teconean Security Force officer, spoke first.

"Officer Kintabi, requesting clearance to the spaceport. General Gandar has requested a complete sweep of the new Federation vessel."

"A trade ship. What could we learn from another trade ship?" barked the security guard, trying to define an importance to his job that would make him superior to a Security Force officer. The SF officers were feared throughout the Teconean Empire. An air of superiority was always expected from one of them, and always resented, though rarely outwardly. Jennifer knew this and had chosen her disguise accordingly. This was the spaceport guard's turf and he would try to show his power to impress the SF officer, but would ultimately back down if challenged.

"Shall I inform Gandar that you think his strategy for sweeping this vessel is a poor one?" she retorted.

He hesitated, but only briefly.

"On the contrary. I think it is wise to sweep it for new technology *in spite* of the fact that it's a mere trade vessel. The Federation is often deceitful. Gandar's wisdom never ceases to amaze me."

"Ah," said Jennifer. "Then you are amazed that Gandar makes these wise decisions."

"No, sir," the guard responded quickly, stumbling over his words. "Of course not. I admire his brilliance and have come to expect his innovative thinking."

"Open the bay doors!" she snapped. "You are delaying my work."

"Yes, sir! Right away."

The transparent doors began to slide apart, and the three of them made their way into the security vestibule. As the doors closed behind them, the heavy steel doors began to slide apart at the other end of the vestibule. Jennifer could feel the seething anger of the Teconean guard who she had just belittled, but he was so frightened of the wrath of an SF officer that he let the three of them pass without formal inspection. He was glad to be rid of them.

They quickly moved from the vestibule into the long dark corridor from which they had entered the day before. As the steel doors shut behind them, they breathed a collective sigh of relief.

"Nice work, Jen."

"Thanks, T.C., but that was the easy part. That old fart's ego was easy to deflate. The young guards of the space dock may be a different story. The fighter pilots guard space dock when they are not on assignment. That way they always have a ready supply of able-bodied pilots standing by in case they have to scuttle ships in an emergency. They love confrontation, and don't scare so easily. Their lives are on the line every time they go up in a starfighter, so they aren't easy to intimidate; there's no cushy job to threaten. I may have a much tougher time talking my way onto the Stargazer."

"It was still a heck of a job, Jen." Danny smiled at her. "It's kinda scary how good an actress you are. I'm starting to wonder just where I do stand with you."

"I don't have to act much with you, Danny," she smiled back with a smile that was deformed through the holoimaging mask.

"All right, you two," T.C. interrupted. "Plenty of time for that later. Let's concentrate on the business at hand."

They headed down the long corridor, lumbering against the strong gravitational pull, silent except for their labored breathing. As they reached the end of the corridor, they felt a faint trembling under their feet.

"A blast?" remarked T.C.. "Who'd be attacking here? The Federation wouldn't launch an attack against Tri-Luna without a working FDS."

"That was no blast, T.C.," Jennifer responded. "It was too sustained, more like a quake."

"A quake! I didn't think there was any tectonic activity on Tri-Luna."

"There's not," Jennifer smiled. "It's got to be the FDS."

"Come again?"

"The FDS is useless without a central core field stabilizer. That's one of the key things that the obelisk allows us to control. If it's not properly calibrated, the result is tectonic destabilization. It's harmless at low power, but at full power it could tear apart the fabric of whatever planet it's located on. The obelisk you brought back…it's useless!" she laughed. "The only reason we would have a tremor here is if they tested the FDS with a faulty obelisk. Of course," the smile left her face "it means that *they* also know that the obelisk is faulty. We don't have much time."

"You don't know the half of it, Jen," Danny muttered.

"What was that, Danny?"

"I'll tell you later, Jen. We'd better get to the Stargazer before this place shuts down."

"Right. Same drill, guys. Ladies first and let me do the talking."

Jennifer led the way down the ramp to the docking bay where the Stargazer was located. The spaceport was sparsely manned in spite of the vast number of ships located there. The main military airbase was on the far side of the spaceport, and most of the arsenal of ships built for the invasion of Earth were there. However, the Stargazer was docked in a smaller bay designed for diplomatic and trade vessels. This was in part to shield the fleet from the prying eyes of traders, who were always willing to sell information for the right price. But it was also for the convenience of the diplomats, who preferred to minimize their walk to the Tri-Luna military base.

Only one guard was stationed at the Stargazer when they arrived. Jennifer led the group directly up to the guard.

"Kintabi, Security Force. I have direct orders from Gandar to sweep this vessel for tech."

She began to walk past him toward the steps.

"Hold it. I've never heard of you. Let's see some I.D."

He held his arm out to block her way, and she barely avoided having his hand penetrate her holofield.

She turned toward him aggressively. "Out of my way. I don't have time for this nonsense. Would you like me to tell Gandar why this sweep was delayed?"

"Go ahead. He'll have my head if I let you in here without checking your I.D.. Would *you* like *me* to tell Gandar that you requested access without an I.D. check?"

She growled at him. "Very well."

She pulled out her counterfeit I.D. and flashed it in front of the guard.

"All right. How did they let a runt like you into the SF anyway?" he quipped. The holoemitter was amazingly lifelike, but couldn't add height to her stature, which was extremely short for a Neanderthal warrior.

"Do not try my patience any further, pilot," she sneered.

The guard backed away, and the three of them walked past him, up to the steps of the Stargazer. As Jennifer stepped up on the first step, another tremor shook the ground. The steps rattled and she lost her footing, falling back into Danny's arms. As she fell back, his arms seemed to go right through her Teconean holoimage body and come to rest on her slim waist. The guard looked on incredulously.

As her holoemitter ring bumped up against Danny's body, the Teconean image faded slightly, and the visage of her slim, human figure was briefly visible. The guard drew his pulse emitter and raised it to fire at Jennifer. T.C. spun, and in a single motion drew his hand phaser and fired at the Teconean guard. His huge body crumpled, and the EM pulse weapon fell harmlessly out of his hand.

Two guards on the far side of the bay heard the commotion and ran toward the Stargazer with their weapons drawn.

"Hurry, guys," yelled T.C.. "No time to get intimate."

Two EM blasts rattled against the steps of the Stargazer, narrowly missing Danny's head. He and Jennifer untangled from each other and hurried up the steps of the ship as T.C. tried to provide cover.

"Move it, T.C.!" Danny yelled from the door of the Stargazer. He leaned out to provide cover as Jennifer ran forward to the bridge to power up the engines.

T.C. hurled his powerful body up the steps and through the door of the ship. "Let's go!" he yelled. "We're in."

"Right" Jennifer yelled back. "Release the docking clamps as soon as you have power."

She fired up the thruster engines as Danny sealed the door, and released the docking clamps. The ship rocked gently once the clamps were off, as the EM pulses pounded the ship. The energy blasts echoed harmlessly off of the external shell of the Stargazer, but they knew they wouldn't be able to stand the force of Teconean blasters once the ground troops arrived. They each took their positions: Danny at the helm, T.C. at weapons, and Jennifer at navigation.

Danny engaged the thrusters and maneuvered the ship off of the ground and toward the massive spaceport security doors through which all ships entered and exited.

"The doors are closed, Danny!" Jennifer screamed. "It's the only way out. We'll have to blast them. Phasers will never penetrate, we'll have to torpedo them and hope the shock wave doesn't ground us."

"Arm the torpedoes, T.C.."

"Already on it, buddy."

They were moving toward the doors, now only about one hundred meters away.

"Now would be a good time!" Danny yelled, the anxiety growing in his usually calm voice.

T.C. fired two torpedoes at the docking doors. They struck thunderously, rocking the Stargazer. Danny struggled to keep the ship in the air and guided it toward the flames up ahead. As the flames began to clear, Danny spotted a small oblong opening in the center of the doors at a forty-five degree angle. He estimated that it was just large enough for the Stargazer to fit through if he could keep the ship at the proper angle.

"Hold on, everybody."

Danny disengaged the autopilot navigational control and activated the rear thrusters. He navigated the ship toward the small opening created by the torpedo blasts, and tilted the Stargazer at a forty-five degree angle. T.C. and Jennifer held on for dear life, struggling to keep from falling out of their seats, unencumbered by the safety belts that they hadn't had time to secure. The ship squeezed through the opening and out into the red Teconean sky. Danny engaged the subthrusters and the Stargazer shot skyward, headed for the outer atmosphere where they could engage impulse engines and plot in a warp drive course for home.

Jennifer spun around toward him. "What are you doing, Danny? We've got to stay low and make a pass over the FDS so that we can take it out."

"Sorry, Jen, but I'm getting us out of here. We've got to get back to Earth before they blow us out of the sky."

"We've got company folks. Four Teconean fighters just launched," said T.C..

Jennifer's harsh gaze never left Danny's face. "I can't believe you. Have you changed that much? The Danny I fell in love with would never have put his own life before the survival of the Federation."

"There are things you don't understand, Jen. No time to explain now. We've got to get out of here in one piece."

The ship rocked as a phaser blast from one of the Teconean fighters hit the ship. T.C. locked and fired on one of the fighters, and it burst into flames.

"One down, three to go. Shields are down twenty-five percent."

"Danny, change course," Jennifer said with more determination in her voice. "That's a direct order. I still outrank you."

"Got ya!" T.C. yelled as he shot down another fighter. "Two down, two to go."

Danny continued to guide the Stargazer to orbital altitude. The ship was rocked again.

"Direct hit," T.C. reported. "Shields are still holding but are down seventy percent. We can't take too many more hits, Danny."

"I said," Jennifer spat out the words sternly "change course, Captain."

Danny glanced over and saw Jennifer standing over him with a hand phaser pointed at him. He turned back to the navigational controls.

"For God's sake, Jen, if you're going to shoot, shoot. There's no time for this now. That FDS is not active, and we've got to get back to the Federation with the Stargazer. This time, *you've* got to show a little trust in *me*. Once I get us out of here, I'll explain everything."

Jennifer stood motionless for a moment, then slowly lowered the phaser. "It wasn't turned on anyway," she said dejectedly. "You'd better have a damn good reason, Danny. Now get us the hell out of here."

The ship was jolted by another blast.

"Shields are down, Danny!"

"We're clear of gravitational forces," Jennifer said. "You've got impulse power."

Danny engaged impulse and started pulling rapidly away from the Teconean fighters.

"Plot us a warp course back to Earth quickly, Jen. Those fighters will be free of gravitational pull and back in weapons range in half a minute."

"I can't. That last blast must have knocked out the space-warp navigational control. We'll have to go on impulse."

"Not for long," T.C. countered. "Those fighters will be free of gravity in fifteen seconds. With our warp drive out, they'll be on us in no time, and we're sitting ducks without our shields."

"Hope you're a good shot, buddy."

"Not good enough to shoot down two of them before they get a shot off."

"No confidence, T.C.. That's always been your problem, no confidence. I'm open to other suggestions."

"Time-warp," Jennifer said. "We can't outrun them, but we can put a few years between us."

The two men spun around to look at her.

"I thought you said the warp system was out."

"The *space-warp* system," Jennifer corrected. "The space-warp navigational array is out, but the warp core power supply is intact. The time-warp system uses the same power source, but uses a totally different navigational array and warp field emitter."

"They're through!" T.C. yelled. "We've got two fighters after us again. Without warp, they'll be on us in fifteen seconds."

"Do it, Jen!"

"I need time. If I don't plot a time course to compensate for the position of the stars and planets in the year we're going to, we'll have no way of knowing what their positions will be. We could warp right into the center of a star. We'd be dead before we completed the time jump."

"Ten seconds," T.C. called out. "Whatever you're going to do, you'd better do it fast."

"But I don't have the time to…"

"Do it **now**, Jen!"

"Five seconds till weapons range!"

"Engaged!" yelled Jennifer. "Grab a hold of something, I don't know when, or *where*, we're going to end up."

They gritted their teeth and grimaced holding tightly to their chairs. The unmistakable sensation of disorientation overcame them as the time-warp system engaged. An eerie stillness overcame them as their senses began to return to normal.

"Well?" Danny asked.

T.C. checked his scanners.

"Nothing out there. I guess it worked."

"Of course it worked," said Jennifer.

"The question is, *when* are we?" asked Danny.

Jennifer checked the navigational scanners on the time-warp navigational array.

"1849. I didn't have time to plot a course. I had to rely on the computer's memory, and the last course plotted other than 2497 was the course Beck had plotted to take you guys back to the Old West—1849."

The three of them burst into laughter, with the sudden release of tension.

"Great," T.C. said. "Just what I wanted, another chance to ride horses and eat dust."

"Not to worry, cowboy," Jennifer replied. "The closest horse is a few million miles from here. Without warp drive, I'd say you're a good six months from a horse."

"Yeah," Danny said "I guess we'd better get to work on that drive, or the Federation will be destroyed before we get back home."

"Forget it," Jennifer said. "We don't have the parts to fix the space-warp navigational system, and the closest Federation outpost from here is on Earth. No, I'm afraid were not getting back home for quite some time. Might as well relax and enjoy the ride boys. It's going to be awfully quiet out here for the next six months. Remember, space travel hasn't been invented yet in this part of the universe."

T.C. rocked back in his chair dejectedly. "But by the time we get back to Earth the Teconeans will have destroyed the Federation. You saw what was going on back there. They were ready to launch a full-scale strike. There must have been a thousand fighters docked in that bay."

"You just don't get it, do you, T.C.?" Jennifer said shaking her head. "You've got to think fourth-dimensionally. We have all of the time in the universe—*literally*—to get back to Earth and warn them. We've still got time-warp control. We'll get back to Earth with hundreds of years to spare. All we have to do is to warp back to the future when we get there. To the folks back home, it'll be like we were never away. In fact, that's what I'm afraid of. It'll be too much like we were never away since you decided to leave that obelisk back there on Tri-Luna, Danny. How could you do that? Not only do we not have it, but the Teconeans are probably sitting on a more advanced version of it than Quigley's got back in the Omnicenter lab. If they can get it to work, the Federation's doomed. I just don't understand how you could take that chance. I know you're not in love with the Space Corps, but that life of yours that you worked so hard to save won't be worth much if the Teconeans invade."

"Take it easy, Jen," Danny said motioning to her to calm down with a gentle downward gesture of his outstretched hands. "Come on back to my quarters with me."

She looked over at Danny indignantly. "Yeah, right! Like you've got a chance! You're not the Danny Stryker who I fell in love with, not by a long shot."

"All right, all right. I'll go back myself. Just wait here."

"I wasn't planning on going anywhere," she quipped motioning to the small confines of the ship.

Danny shook his head and headed back to his quarters.

"What's gotten into him, T.C.? How did Danny get like this?"

"He's got to have a good reason, Jen. Danny would never put his own life before the Federation. Heck, his biggest problem is that he never seems to put his own life before much of anything. If Danny believes in something, he charges in headfirst. I'm the practical one. Danny's got the passion, and I'm the one who's always pulling him back to reality."

"I don't know, T.C.. It sure doesn't look that way to me." Jennifer slumped down in her chair, fraught with the disappointment that she felt in her heart. "I thought that this time we might really make it work."

The two of them sat in silence. Jennifer in despair and T.C. frustrated with his inability to reassure her. He knew his friend well. He knew that Danny wouldn't even think about his own safety if the alternative meant damaging the Federation. There had to be an explanation. T.C. feared that the explanation was Jennifer. Danny might have let his judgment get clouded by the thought of endangering Jennifer's life if he had stayed to destroy the Teconean FDS.

"Here," said Danny walking out on to the bridge again. "Here is the reason that we needed to get out of there," he said, waving the obelisk above his head. "Look at you two! No confidence. Man, have a little faith in a guy, would you."

Jennifer looked up. "I don't understand, Danny."

"Of course you don't. That's the point."

"What is that?" asked T.C.. "I don't get it. Where'd you get that one from?"

"Quigley," Danny replied. "That clever old coot suspected all along that Beck might try to sabotage us, and as much as he believes in you, Jen, he wanted an extra safeguard just in case."

"You mean...," she started.

"Yeah, exactly," said Stryker. "Don't look so hurt. It was nothing personal. You wouldn't be putting your pride ahead of the survival of the Federation's now, would you?" he said slyly.

"All right, all right," she said, letting down her defenses. "So what did you do, Danny? That's the real one, isn't it?"

"Yeah, this is the one we brought back with us," he said holding it out for her to look at. "The one you gave the Neanders was the one that Quigley gave me. I slipped that into the saddlebag back in the nineteenth century when I got back to the ship, and tucked this one away safely in the false compartment under my bunk. When you came into the Stargazer with your boyfriend Hans, you grabbed Quigley's obelisk out of my saddlebag."

"My *boyfriend*? A bit jealous, are we?"

"Well, what can I say? You got real bad taste."

"All right, we can do this later."

"I look forward to it."

"So what's the deal, Danny?" interrupted T.C.. "Is this the real thing, or what? Is that obelisk in your hand going to activate the FDS?"

"I don't know, buddy. We won't know until we get back and let Quigley have a look at it. But I do know that that one Jennifer gave Beck to slip into the Neanders' FDS won't work. In fact, it'll likely destroy the whole damn planet."

"What? How?"

"Quigley programmed that thing to fuse itself into the FDS once inserted. They won't be able to get it out without destroying the whole thing, which they won't be too anxious to do after all of the work and bribes it took to build it. And if they don't get it out of there in time, the system will progressively destabilize, increasing the tectonic activity until it rips the planet apart. Either way, they're not going to have a functional FDS for a long, long time."

"That should buy the Federation some time, then. The Neanders are aggressive, but they've never been willing to take on the Federation's technological edge."

"Don't be so sure, T.C.," Danny replied. "If they suspect that we got away with a working version of the obelisk, then we may have just started a war. Gandar knows that the Teconeans have no chance of taking Earth once the FDS is activated. If he suspects that the Federation is close to activating the system, then he'll launch the invasion even if he doesn't have his FDS working."

"*Especially* if his FDS isn't working," Jennifer said.

The two men looked over at her curiously.

"Why especially?" asked T.C.. "The Teconeans rarely go into battle without a tactical advantage"

"Because that monkey wrench that Quigley threw into their plans with the bogus obelisk will set their project back at least a year. They'll have to destroy their FDS in order to keep Tri-Luna from self-destructing, a chance they'd never take with such a large armada of attack ships at stake. And once they realize the extent of the damage, I don't think they'll be too concerned about whether or not we got away with a working version of the obelisk. They'll be so far behind Omnicenter in development that they'll know they could never hope to have the system working before the Federation does. An attack is imminent."

"Great!" T.C. threw up his hands in frustration. "And we're stuck back here in the nineteenth century with the one thing that could save the Federation."

"Right," Danny continued, "but with all of the time in the universe to get back there and save the day. We can just cruise on back to Earth at our leisure, then when we get there we time-warp back to the twenty-fifth century and install the obelisk. Heck, we can even go back a few years early and give Quigley a chance to make sure the thing works."

"No," said Jennifer. "We can't go back early. We'd risk distorting the timeline. We can't go back until *after* we left there. Otherwise there would be two of each of us on Earth at the same time. God knows what might happen. We could end up altering the timeline in a way that insures the Teconeans victory. Beck or one of the other Teconean moles could spot us and tip off the Teconeans to our time travel capabilities. That could be enough to start the attack before Quigley can even test the new obelisk. Or worse yet, Beck might steal it from us and get it to Gandar."

"Then why don't we just warp back to the twenty-first century and warn people about the Teconeans before they ever leave the Himalayas? We can contain the problem before it even starts. There will never even *be* a Teconean Empire."

"Bad idea again, Danny," Jennifer answered. "We can't just mess with the space time continuum."

"Sometimes rules are made to be broken, Jen. We can manipulate the continuum to our advantage and save billions of lives."

"It's dangerous to play God, Danny. There are just too many variables to know the consequences that our actions would bring. The only thing we know for sure is that things would not be the same when we get back, and personally I like the future we were living in."

"A future on the brink of war?"

"Well, at least we know where we stand and who we're up against. Think back to your history lessons. When outworld colonization started, the planets each developed their own governments and economies. There was tremendous dissension among the outworlds, and they each resented Earth for the control it exerted on them. We were all going in different directions—entropy at work. It wasn't until the ubiquitous threat of a Teconean Empire attack on humankind that the outworlds and Earth agreed to accept a common government at Omnicenter and a unified Space Corps for the protection of the Federation. If it hadn't been for the Teconeans, Earth may well have been at war with the outworlds by the twenty-fifth century. If we prevent the Neanders from leaving the Himalayas in the twenty-first century, who knows what will await us when we get back to the twenty-fifth century?"

"I hate those timeline paradox things," T.C. said. "Let's leave well enough alone and get home. Like you say, there's no rush to get back. We'll travel on impulse power and get a chance to catch up on some reading. I can't remember the last time I had a vacation."

"I hate to rain on your parade, pal, but what's a vacation without food?"

"Don't you guys have a hydroponics bay on the Stargazer? That's supposed to be mandatory for all Federation vessels in case you get stranded out in space. The emergency rations will run out before we're half way home."

"What, are you kidding? Look at this ship. Where would we set up a hydroponics bay? We use every spare inch of this tub for cargo storage space. I've got to make a living, you know. I'm not usually running around trying to save the universe."

"You broke down your hydroponics bay for storage space!" yelled Jennifer. "What are you guys, nuts? How are we going to get back home?"

"You're the scientist," Danny said sheepishly. "You think of something."

Jennifer was furious. She was a stickler for protocol, and it always got under her skin the way Danny twisted the rules to meet his own needs. But that was one of the things she admired at the same time. He was incredibly resourceful.

"Don't look at me, wonder boy. This is your game."

"Wait a minute!" T.C. broke in. "When was the original Orion settlement abandoned?"

Danny looked over at him with an annoyed expression on his face. "What could that possibly have to do…"

"Of course!" Jennifer interrupted, her eyes lighting up as she realized what T.C. was getting at. "When they originally settled Tri-Luna, the first thing they did was build a large hydroponics lab so they would have ample food supplies for the arriving colonists who they had hoped would come to build the colony. Although the settlement was never a success, the food lab worked perfectly. We all learned about it in school because it became the prototype for hydroponics labs for all later space exploration and settlement."

"Right," continued T.C. with a smile of satisfaction, "and if I remember my history right, the food production was a lot more successful than the colonization effort. By the time the colony was abandoned, the hydroponics lab was producing more food than they could eat. It was too expensive to dismantle the lab and take it back to Earth, so they left it there. Enough food to feed a small city on a planet that had no advanced life forms."

"Brilliant, T.C.," said Danny. "See, Jen, no problem."

"I guess I've got some work to do," she said.

Jennifer checked the computer records for the date the colony had been abandoned, and began working to plot a time course to go back to Tri-Luna three days after the settlers had departed. She figured that no one would be in the area to detect the Stargazer by then, and the ion storms of Orion would shield them from Earth's long range scans. It seemed like a reasonable plan, one they could pull off without risking detection that might interrupt the timeline. They would stop off in the twenty-second century and pick up supplies before returning back to the nineteenth century, a time when they could make the trip back to Earth undetected.

*   *   *   *   *   *   *   *

The Teconean attack vessels returned to Tri-Luna, and the pilots were greeted by Gandar and Hans Beck.

"Well?" demanded Gandar.

"Two ships lost, sir."

"To a cargo ship!" Gandar was furious. "How do you expect to win a war if you can't defeat a cargo ship piloted by a trader?"

"He's no trader," Beck said. "Stryker's a retired Space Corps captain, and the best pilot in the Fleet in his day, except for me."

"Silence, human!" Gandar snapped. He turned back to the pilots. "What of the cargo vessel?"

"Destroyed, sir. We saw the explosion. It was massive—a brilliant flash of light and a sonic burst that shook our ship. They must have been carrying weapons."

"Did you see any debris?" asked Beck.

Gandar began to growl, but Beck interrupted before he could protest. Beck was not easily intimidated.

"Forgive the intrusion, Gandar. I do not mean to get in the way of your interrogation of your men, but bear with me a moment. There are things you do not yet know of Federation technology."

"Very well. Speak."

"Did you see any debris?" he again asked the pilots.

"No," they grunted, offended at being interrogated by a human. "As we stated, the explosion was massive. There was nothing left."

"Perhaps the obelisk caused the explosion when our torpedoes hit their vessel" said Gandar.

"Perhaps," Beck said, "but there is a more worrisome possibility. Even a massive explosion would be likely to leave behind some debris from the ship. If, however, there was no explosion…"

"You dare to question the integrity of an imperial fighter pilot!" roared one of the pilots.

Gandar held up his right hand and motioned his warrior not to attack.

"Of course not," Beck responded quickly. "Teconean warriors are the most honorable that history has ever known. I know better than to question your integrity, Captain. However, you may well have been duped by the Stargazer's time-warp field."

"Beck!" shouted Gandar. He spun and shot the two warriors before they could even muster up an expression of surprise. "We agreed not to discuss time-warp outside of the high military command center. If my men even suspected that a Space Corps vessel was capable of time-warp, they would lose their nerve. They would never carry off the attack against Earth. Now that the Stargazer is destroyed, we may still have time to rebuild the FDS and get it operational before the Federation does."

"It's not destroyed," said Beck dryly.

"What? My men said that…"

"They said that they saw a brilliant flash of light accompanied by a sonic burst—the kind of phenomenon that occurs when a ship engages time-warp drive. That's what they saw. If they had seen an explosion, there would have been debris."

"So. They escaped in time. If they have the obelisk, they can deliver it to the Federation at any time. For all we know, the FDS at Omnicenter could already be operational."

"Not likely," Beck said. "I don't think they would risk going back to Earth before today. It would risk disrupting the timeline, and Dr. Lee knows better than to take that kind of chance. No, they are on their way there as we speak. I'm sure of it."

"Then we have no time to waste," Gandar said emphatically. "We must launch the attack today. We cannot risk the time it would take to rebuild the FDS. The Federation must be destroyed before they activate their FDS. Agreed?"

"Agreed."

Gandar drew his weapon and fired point blank at the human who he had tolerated out of need, but had never respected. Beck had a curious look on his face as he clutched his chest and glanced up at Gandar.

"Then I guess we have no need of you anymore, traitor," muttered Gandar as Beck crumpled lifelessly to the floor.

* * * * * * * *

The three crewmembers of the Stargazer stared anxiously at their viewscreens as the ship approached Tri-Luna. It was a much different scene than the one they had left only a few hours earlier. There was the same beautiful red hue, but the military base was gone. The planet's surface was pristine. They scanned the terrain for evidence of the small colony the Earth settlers had abandoned just a few days before.

"It's beautiful," said Jennifer. "I never really appreciated the beauty of Tri-Luna from the bridge of a Teconean vessel."

"It still gives me the creeps," T.C. said.

"Yeah," Danny said, "but somehow it seems a lot more peaceful knowing there's no Neanders here."

"I've got it on the scanners, guys," said Jennifer. "It's not much of a colony, but there it is, right where the Teconean base will be built a couple of hundred years from now. Landing course plotted in."

"Right," acknowledged Danny. "Heading in."

T.C.'s face lit up. "Hey, as long as we're down there, why don't we plant some mines under the area where the Teconeans will build the military spaceport. We could warp back to the twenty-fifth century and blow them to oblivion before they ever launch the attack. That'll give the Federation plenty of time to prepare, even if this new obelisk doesn't work."

"T.C.," Jennifer started in, "I thought we went through all this."

"Uh oh. Here we go again." Danny rolled his eyes.

Jennifer gave him a dirty look, and turned back toward T.C.. "If we lay those mines, how do we know for sure who might find them and whether one might go off before we trigger them? We've got more than two hundred years for something to go wrong. We can't risk disrupting the timeline."

"Yeah, yeah. I get it, but it sure is tempting."

"Prepare for landing," said Danny. "Let's go get some food."

They landed the Stargazer near the abandoned settlement and made their way out toward the hydroponics bay. As expected, supplies were plentiful. They stocked the Stargazer's food bays with enough food for the long trip back to Earth.

The Stargazer took off from Tri-Luna, and warped back to the nineteenth century. Danny, T.C. and Jennifer settled into the Stargazer for the long journey. During the next six months, they renewed the friendships the three of them had had during their days at the Academy. Danny was uncertain about how the forced intimacy would affect the renewed romance that he and Jennifer were experiencing. Much to his surprise, the relationship fit like a glove. They enjoyed each other's company more and more with each passing day, and the romance that had withered several years before began to flourish. By the time that they began to approach Earth's solar system, they were both sorry to see the voyage coming to an end. Though truly in love, they were afraid to talk of the future. Their life on Earth had torn their future apart once before.

They remained in the nineteenth century until they were able to obtain orbit around Earth. Jennifer then plotted a course for 2497. The three of them said good-bye to their six-month vacation and prepared for the jump.

CHAPTER XXI

Back to the Future Again

"Identify your vessel immediately or you will be destroyed. I repeat, identify yourselves immediately."

The three time travelers slowly came out of the disorienting fog of their time-warp, shaken back into reality by the warning coming through their comm port from Space Corps Command.

"Damn! I'll never get used to that feeling," Danny said. "Stargazer" he said to the Space Corps security guard. "Trade vessel returning from Teconean space. Captain Danny Stryker."

"Why didn't your approach show up on our scanners?"

Danny was not in the mood for protocol. "Don't know, doughboy. I guess you'd better check your equipment. Your commander's going to have your ass when you tell him you didn't pick us up until we were in orbit."

"Uh. Right. Knew you were there all the time, Stargazer. Just pulling your chain. You're clear to land."

T.C. laughed. "Give the kid a break, Danny. It's probably his first watch. He'll be sweating like a pig all night wondering whether you're going to turn him in."

"Just having some fun, man. You know, one last time before we yank ourselves back into reality. I'm going to miss the solitude of the nineteenth century. No comm links, no Teconean fighter pilots, no Space Corps regs."

"I hear ya, buddy, but the vacation's over. Now that we're back, time is of the essence. As soon as Gandar realizes that we got away, he'll probably send the starfighter fleet based on Tri-Luna to attack Earth as quickly as possible. The only thing that was holding them back was the promise of completing the FDS before the Federation did. That hope vanished as soon as Quigley's false obelisk destroyed the prototype FDS copy Beck had built for them."

The Stargazer landed in space dock without further incident, and the three explorers made their way directly to Omnicenter. They placed an urgent call to General Thompson who met them at the main security entrance. He had a look of grave concern on his face.

"What's the matter, General?"

"Ever since you told us of your 'incident' in the Orion system, Danny, I've had Ski keep close sensor tabs on that sector. About an hour ago, just as you were making your approach to space dock, we picked up massive activity emanating from there. The ion storms of Orion limit our ability to pinpoint the nature of that activity, of course, but the time lapse scans show a pattern indicative of a growing armada. My suspicion is that they're amassing an attack fleet. That could only mean that they've beat us to the punch in the completion of the FDS."

"Or that they believe that we're about to beat them to the punch," Danny said.

Thompson looked up at Danny and paused for a moment, letting Danny's thought sink in. "Then you've got it?" he asked Danny.

"Sure hope so."

"We've got *something*, anyway," Jennifer said. "We just don't know if it's any better than what we've already tried. There was no way to test the obelisk that Danny brought back from the nineteenth century."

"What are you doing here anyway, Dr. Lee?" I thought you were taking off to visit with your family while these fellows were gallivanting back in time with Beck." He glanced around. "And speaking of Beck, where is he? If your suspicions about him were correct, Dr. Lee, we shouldn't let him out of our sight at a time like this."

"It's a long story, General, but I don't think we have to worry about Beck anymore. I imagine the Teconeans took care of that for us."

Thompson looked up at her with a confused expression on his face. From his time perspective, Beck had just left on the Stargazer a few days before with Stryker and McGee. The plan had been for them to retrieve the obelisk, and then return to the twenty-fifth century a few minutes after they had left. When they didn't return on schedule, Thompson assumed that something had gone wrong. He had consoled Jennifer who had acted equally surprised at their absence. She neglected to tell Thompson of Beck's plan to divert the Stargazer back to Tri-Luna after they had retrieved the obelisk, and meet her at the Teconean base on Tri-Luna. She was afraid, and rightly so, that Thompson would never let her go alone to Tri-Luna, and she knew that if she showed up with any-one else her cover would be blown and the mission would be doomed to failure. So instead, she feigned terrible grief at Danny's loss, and had told Thompson that she was going to visit with family on Kennedy Prime, the first outworld settled by humans, which was named for the father of the American space program. Thompson had no idea that she had been on Tri-Luna, and had just placed an urgent e-mail to Jennifer when the activity in the Orion system was reported.

"We'd better get a move on, General. I'll explain on the way."

Thompson seethed in silent anger as Jennifer's story unfolded. He was furious that she had kept him in the dark, but at the same time, he admired her gumption. He was just as embarrassed as he was angry, annoyed at himself for not having seen through her plans. *But then again*, he thought, *those eyes could melt away any man's reason, even mine.*

"That Stryker is one lucky fellow," he muttered under his breath, not realizing that his thoughts were becoming audible.

"Excuse me, sir?" Jennifer said. "I didn't catch that."

"Uh, nothing. Just thinking out loud, Doctor," he said, loosening his collar as he felt the blush that his dark skin thankfully concealed from the others.

"So, you've got the obelisk then?"

"Yes, sir, but we still don't know if it's a functional version. We only know that it's more advanced than the ones we've made so far. I can tell from the prototype number that Quigley engraves on the base."

"It better be functional, or we're in for a real bloodbath."

The Teconean warriors had no respect for the rules of the Geneva Convention. Those were human rules, and they had no use for them. Teconeans were notoriously brutal warriors.

The four of them made their way through Omnicenter toward the research lab. Unlike their last time here, the hallways were bustling with activity. Everyone seemed frantic to get where they were going. There had never been a state of alert in Omnicenter during the lifetime of any of these people, and the tension was obvious.

They greeted Quigley, who had been alerted to their arrival shortly after Thompson had learned that they were back. Danny pulled the obelisk out of his saddlebag and handed it to the professor.

Quigley studied it carefully, noting, as had Jennifer, that the engraving it bore marked it as more advanced than any model yet developed. "Very promising. Very promising."

"Sir," came a voice from the comm link. Danny recognized Ski's voice right away.

"Hey, Ski! How's it goin'?"

"Not so great, Danny, but glad to hear you made it back okay. Sorry to interrupt, General, but we now have a clear picture on our long-range scanners. I think you'd better take a look."

"Patch it through to the main view screen down here, would you?"

"Sure thing, sir."

The scanning grid appeared on the view screen on the far wall of the lab. They all recognized the pattern of a massive array of ships moving toward Earth at warp speed.

"Good God! How much time do you figure we have, Ski?"

"Approximately fifteen minutes until they get close enough to drop out of warp. Maybe another ten minutes after that until they pass Jupiter and begin scattering into an attack pattern." He paused briefly. "I figure we've got about thirty-five, forty minutes tops before they're in firing range. If the FDS isn't active by then we're sitting ducks unless we've got fighters in the air."

"Thanks," said Thompson. "Keep me posted."

"General!" said Danny. "What are you waiting for? We've got to get the Starfighter Fleet airborne or we're dead."

Thompson looked over at Quigley.

"No guarantee, sir," Quigley responded to the unasked question. "I need time to study it. If it's a decoy like the one I sent to Tri-Luna, it could destroy the whole FDS."

"I know scientists don't like risk, they like to study until a point of certainly, or at least probability, exists that can assure the desired outcome. Unfortunately, military leaders and politicians don't always have that luxury. Quigley, my man, you've just made the jump from scientist to politician."

"No need for insults, sir. Present company excepted, of course."

"Of course," Thompson chuckled. "The point is, this is one of those situations when we don't have the luxury of time to study our options. Insert the obelisk."

"General!" Danny interrupted again. "Either way, why risk being caught with our pants down? Let's get some starfighters up there."

"Bad idea, Captain," Quigley answered. "If the FDS does work, it'll disable any ship in its field, even ours. If we're going to have any chance, we've got to hope that this thing works," he said holding up the obelisk.

"We're still going to need to have our starfighters intact to secure the area afterwards."

"Now you're thinking like a military strategist," Thompson said to Quigley.

"Thanks," he grunted.

Quigley got to work immediately. He carefully inserted the new obelisk into the FDS, and the magnetic seal sucked it into place with a solid-sounding "swoosh." He started the sequence to power up the obelisk and begin its calibration. "This is going to take some time," he said to the others, who were all staring over his shoulders in anticipation. "Why don't you go sit down?"

"Are you kidding?" T.C. said. "I can't relax at a time like this."

"Well, maybe I can," Quigley said, with a bit of annoyance in his voice. "At least enough to do my job anyway. Give me some air, folks. Would you?"

They walked away, feeling rather useless with nothing they could do to help other than staying out of Quigley's way. They all looked on from a distance.

"Just what does that thing do anyway, Jen? Why is it so hard to design and calibrate an energy field core stabilizer? It sounds like something that should be pretty basic for a guy like Quigley."

"Well," she started, "calling it a core stabilizer is a bit misleading really. When we started work on it, we were afraid of what would happen if word leaked out about what we were really working on. The implications are astounding, actually. We all decided to call it a core stabilizer, but it's really much more than that. If you really found a functional model of the obelisk back in time, then you've made the greatest discovery of the twenty-fifth century—a nutonium stream accelerator."

"A what?

"A nutonium stream accelerator."

"Yeah, I heard you the first time, but what is it?"

"Well, as we neared completion of the FDS, we ran into two major problems. The first was the sheer size of the field that we'd have to generate to protect an entire planet. It would take a tremendous amount of nutonium to produce the power needed for the FDS using traditional nutonium fission generators. Running a field the size of the planet would deplete our nutonium supplies too quickly. We thought about protecting just the starships with smaller field generators, but even for a field that size, the generator needed to produce adequate power to maintain an active FDS field would be too bulky to fit on a starship. We had to come up with a much smaller, more efficient energy source. To solve the problem, Quigley developed a compact energy source.

"A nutonium stream accelerator," Danny interrupted.

"Right," Jennifer continued. "By last year, Quigley had solved the puzzle of how to increase the power generated by nutonium fission, and how to make it compact enough to be practical even for a starship. He developed this theory of power amplification that assumes that rapid acceleration of the nutonium particles prior to fission should increase the energy release a hundred fold. The problem is accelerating the particles in a controlled manner. If done en masse, it could generate so much force that the energy release could not be contained. Not only would it be useless, but it would cause a massive explosion. The answer, he theorized, was to organize the nutonium particles in a stream made up of single nutonium particles flowing in a straight line. They could then be accelerated one particle at a time and released in controlled fission as a usable energy source."

"Unfortunately, though, all our designs had the same problem—a fluctuation in the energy signature yielded by the fission. That was the second problem, the one we haven't solved yet. The challenge was to develop a system that would accelerate the particles in a controlled fashion. If the precise rate of the stream flow is not maintained, then the energy fluctuates. Even a slight fluctuation will induce harmonic variations in the FDS fields. That, in turn, can cause tectonic activity in the planet within the field. In other words, the unstable energy supply leads to an unstable FDS. We'd risk destroying Earth if we used it. We're so close to solving it, but now…"

"So the obelisk is some kind of a power source?"

"Yes," Jennifer answered. "Unlike any we've ever known. And the implications are Earth-shattering."

She hesitated as she realized what she had said, and they all burst out laughing. "Bad metaphor," she said. "What I meant was that this discovery could change the future course of humanity. It would be the most efficient energy source ever developed. Not only would it allow our ships to travel with only a fraction of the mass of fuel they need now, but it could be used to power Earth and all the outworlds on one one-hundredth of the nutonium we now require. The mines of Andromeda IV could supply the whole Federation. Our dependence on the nutonium mines of Teconea would be a thing of the past. As I said, this would be the most important discovery of the twenty-fifth century."

"Fifteen minutes until they're within weapons range," Ski's voice boomed out overhead.

Jennifer paused and looked over anxiously at the professor. Thompson started to walk over to check on his progress.

"Not now, General," he said, without looking up.

Thompson hesitated, then decided to stay out of Quigley's way. He headed back to the group.

Once again Jennifer ignored the interruption and went on with her explanation, as much to occupy her nervous mind as to answer Danny's questions. "Thus far, we haven't been able to come up with a model that holds the calibration settings precisely enough to maintain an even nutonium stream acceleration. The professor's latest attempt involves a series of incremental accelerators within the obelisk, rather than a single accelerator. If we can find the right number and sequence of particle acceleration speeds, we should be able to achieve a stable stream speed. Our last model was darn close, that's why I believe that any future model you may have found will be advanced enough to likely be the one that works. Hopefully," she said, pointing to the obelisk that Quigley was working on, "that's it."

"Ten minutes until weapons range," came Ski's voice booming over the comm system.

For the first time in his life, Danny thought, Ski's voice was beginning to get really irritating.

Jennifer paused for a moment, and then resumed her explanation. "You see, the central core of the obelisk contains seven small spheres arranged in a linear fashion from the tip of the obelisk to its base. Inside each of these spheres is a thin metallic wafer, coated on opposite halves of each side with a thin layer of gold. When a microcurrent is applied to the wafers, it causes them to spin. The rate of spin of each wafer can be varied by the amount of current applied to it. The spinning wafer then induces a magnetic field around the sphere; the faster the spin rate, the stronger the magnetic field. By varying the current to each sphere individually, they can each be calibrated to have a different magnetic field strength. Each sphere is individually shielded from the others to keep the magnetic fields from interfering with each other. Quigley designed the obelisk so that each sphere can be individually calibrated by an external computer via contacts on the outer surface of the obelisk. Those contacts are the markings that you saw along each side of the obelisk. Each of the seven spheres needs to be calibrated at incrementally increasing spin rates from the tip of the obelisk to the base. A nutonium stream is then directed into the obelisk through the point at the top. As the individual nutonium particles are exposed to the magnetic fields, their speed is accelerated. As it passes from one sphere to the next, the nutonium particle increases its velocity incrementally. By the time it exits near the base, its rate of speed is one hundred times what it was when it entered."

"Five minutes to weapons range."

Thompson turned toward Quigley. "It's now or never, Professor. Is that thing going to work?"

"I've almost got it. I'm just having trouble getting the calibrations to stabilize long enough to…What the heck? Dr. Lee, take a look at this."

"No time for explanations, Professor, I need a yes or no." Thompson opened a comm link, and prepared to launch his starfighters.

"Whoa!" Ski's voice came blasting over the comm. "They've come to a dead stop!"

Thompson delayed the order. "What do you suppose they're up to?" he asked.

"It's the FDS," Danny said matter-of-factly. "They've discovered that we still haven't launched any fighters, and they're wondering if we've found a way to activate the FDS. You see, they have no way to scan for the FDS field. They don't know what the field signature looks like. We've got a brief reprieve, but it won't last long. They won't give up that easy."

"A single Teconean fighter has broken away from the armada," Ski said, "traveling directly toward Earth at one quarter impulse."

"This may be our last window of opportunity, General," Danny said. "Once that ship reaches orbit unharmed, they'll know that the FDS is inactive. We've got to launch now."

"Right, Danny. Open a comm link to the starfighter command base."

"Wait!" shouted Jennifer. She was looking over the professor's shoulder at the obelisk. A faint glow emanated through the clear metal base of the obelisk. In external lighting, the base had appeared to be composed of the same vitanium as the rest of the shell of the obelisk, but once it was powered up, the glow of the internal components in the base showed plainly through the clear metal. The lighted markings consisted of two concentric circles surrounding an opening about one centimeter in diameter. Between the circles were the letters J.L. on the left and D.S. on the right, and the numbers eighteen on the top, and forty-nine on the bottom.

"I've left myself a key!" she said.

Ski's voice interrupted overhead. "Teconean attack vessel has reached orbital distance from Earth and stopped."

"It's now or never, Dr. Lee."

"Danny," she said quickly, "Do you have your six-shooter?"

Danny smiled. "Wouldn't be without it, Jen."

"Get the silver bullet and give it to me now!"

"Teconean armada has resumed course. Thirty seconds to weapons range."

Danny pulled the six-shooter out of his saddlebag, and removed the silver bullet.

"Twenty seconds."

"I've almost got it, General! Hold the Fleet."

She unlocked the clear metal plate and removed it from the base of the obelisk, exposing the glowing insignia surrounding a small chamber in the base of the obelisk.

"Ten seconds."

"God help us," muttered Thompson.

Jennifer slipped the silver bullet into the chamber and secured the clear metal plate.

"The spin calibrations are stabilizing!" shouted Quigley. "That bullet of yours must have activated an energy stabilization circuit within the obelisk. The future Jennifer must have encoded the circuit with…"

"The hell with scientific theory, Professor. Is that thing working or not?" demanded Thompson.

"Five…four…three…two…one…"

They all held their breath and braced for the attack. Omnicenter would certainly be the first target.

"My God!" came Ski's voice over the comm link. Will you look at that? The Teconean ships are spinning around aimlessly like a pile of space debris."

"I guess it's working," said Quigley, stating the obvious.

"Of course!" said Jennifer with an air of discovery. "I'm brilliant!" she said triumphantly as she realized what Quigley was talking about.

"I always was a sucker for a modest girl," Danny laughed.

Jennifer, too proud of herself to notice, ignored Danny's comment. "I must have encoded an energy field stabilizer chip within the obelisk to be activated by a specific sonic wavelength; the wavelength produced by the sonic generator in the silver bullet. That was the key that my future self must have used to assure security in case the obelisk were to be stolen. Even if someone else were to have discovered the receptacle for the bullet, no one but Danny or I would know that it was for the sonic generator I built for Danny's six-shooter, the one shaped like a silver bullet. Only Danny's silver bullet could stabilize the field."

They looked up at the view screen, and saw the lifeless Teconean armada in complete disarray. Most of the ships were spinning aimlessly; those close enough to get pulled into Earth's orbit were beginning to drift away from the rest.

"No energy signatures out there, sir," said Ski. "Shall we begin search and rescue operations?"

"Not just yet," said Thompson. "Not just yet."

General Thompson was not one to savor the suffering of his enemies, but he knew that if he deactivated the field while the Teconeans were still alive, they would attack. He wasn't sure if Earth could survive that attack, and looked on with a sense of deep regret as the powerless ships entombed and suffocated the warriors within.

＊　＊　＊　＊　＊　＊　＊　＊

Gandar was with the third wave of vessels, and watched in horror as one third of his armada was completely destroyed without ever firing a shot. He seethed with anger, and vowed revenge as he reluctantly turned the remainder of his fleet back toward Teconea.

Chapter XXII

Sunset

It had been two weeks since the Teconean invasion, and the pace of life at Omnicenter was finally returning to normal. Commander General Thompson had returned to the drudgery of administrative work, although somehow it didn't seem so bad to him now after the stressful events of recent weeks. He had done his best to convince Danny to return to the Space Corps, and felt pretty good about his chances to win him over now that Danny's lucrative trade routes with the Teconean worlds were cut off. All that was left to do was to sit back and wait for Danny's answer, but he was sure he'd say yes. After all, Danny Stryker was the kind of man who thrived on excitement, and what kind of life could compare with what he had experienced since his return to Earth.

Professor Quigley and Jennifer were hard at work, trying to keep up with the administration's demands for the fabrication of the nutonium accelerators for the Fleet. Jennifer's mind had been elsewhere though, and even Quigley, who rarely concerned himself with the personal lives of those around him, was worried about her. She was spending more time away from the lab than in it. Quigley gladly covered for her, knowing that she needed the time to be with Captain Stryker. Besides, she needed to make peace with herself before her mind would be clear enough to be of much help to him in the lab.

Quigley was a workaholic, but even he had had enough. He had hardly been out of the lab for two weeks and his thoughts were beginning to run together. He decided to make his way up to the outdoor observation deck lounge and have a drink to unwind before taking a much-needed weekend off. The lounge was on the roof of Omnicenter Central, overlooking the spaceport. It was a popular spot for pilots to meet their wives or girlfriends when they were returning from duty, but was usually deserted on Friday evenings. No one wanted to hang out at work on a Friday evening. That's exactly why Quigley liked it. Quigley liked solitude.

He exited the turbolift and opened the doors to the observation deck lounge. There, at the far end of the deck, silhouetted against the bright orange sky, was the unmistakable figure of Jennifer Lee. He was always oblivious to her beauty in the lab, seeing her only as a colleague, but at times like this even he was taken by the sensuality of her presence. Nonetheless, his feelings toward her were more fraternal than anything else. She was one of the few people who could understand his mind, and had always been a dear friend to him. His mind told him that she was best left alone tonight, but the body often betrays the mind. Before he knew it, he found himself standing beside her with his hand reaching out to rest on her shoulder. She looked up at him and smiled, then gazed back toward the spaceport in time to see the Stargazer lift off and fly away into the sunset. Her face was sad and her eyes remained fixed on the horizon long after the ship had disappeared. Quigley gave her a gentle squeeze on the shoulder, then walked back toward the bar next to the observation deck entrance and pulled up a stool.

Jennifer's mind wandered back over the last two weeks. There had been a tremendous sense of relief with the elimination of the Teconean threat, but with that relief came the luxury of time to ponder her life. During the six months that she and Danny had spent back in time on the Stargazer, there was nothing between them but their love, no worries of the direction of their future other than to resolve the immediate threat of the Teconean invasion upon their return to Earth. But once that threat was gone and they were back in the twenty-fifth century, everything was different. They once again faced the dilemma of staying happy with each other without tearing each other from their respective careers. Although the Teconean trade routes were gone for Danny, he still wasn't comfortable with Space Corps life. He could certainly spend more time on Earth now that his trade routes would be limited to the Federation, but it would still mean a lot of time away from Jennifer. She had hoped to persuade him that the less lucrative trade routes of the Federation weren't worth the hard life of a trader always in transit between worlds, but she knew in her heart that a sedentary job on Earth would never make him happy.

It had been a difficult two weeks. She and Danny tried to maintain the lighthearted relationship that they had enjoyed aboard the Stargazer, but without success. The day before had been a beautiful day, and Danny had taken her for a walk in Rinfeld Park. They had meandered up the azalea path hand in hand and reveled in the last blooms of the fading mums splashing their bright yellow color against the browning background of the withering plants. He had held her tightly and kissed her with a feeling of total symbiosis, and at that moment she realized that, despite the indestructible bond between their souls, he was leaving. It was a moment she would never forget.

Quigley watched from the bar as Jennifer's silhouette faded gradually into the darkening crimson sunset, and eventually disappeared into the blackness of night as the sun drifted over the horizon. Her body never moved as she stared out into her past and pondered her future. She smiled as a tear rolled down her cheek, knowing that somehow their love would endure.

*   *   *   *   *   *   *   *

and now, a glimpse at…

The Starscape Project

The *Stargazer* inched gradually closer to the Teconean starfighter with each passing minute, but they were closing the gap with excruciating slowness. The crew of the *Stargazer* had completed their preparations, with the help of the tactical information that Blake had provided. There was little to do now but wait.

Jennifer gazed out of the one true window on the ship, a small porthole in the hallway between the sleeping quarters and the control room. With spacewarp engaged, the stars passed by quickly, but it was still a breathtaking sight. The computer viewscreen was easier to use for navigation, adjusting it to display the view from virtually any vantage point around the *Stargazer*. It gave a much more comprehensive view of the space around the ship, but one that was not nearly as beautiful as the real thing. Danny walked up beside her, and put his arm around her. She glanced over at him briefly, and then returned her gaze to the stars, a smile of comfort still on her face.

"Sometimes I forget how beautiful it really is out here," he said.

Jennifer's gaze stayed fixed on the passing stars. "You guys take this for granted, but for me…" her voice trailed off as she stood motionless, staring out the window, and sighed. Jennifer spent most of her time in the lab at Omnicenter. Even though she was a Space Corps officer, her opportunities to actually travel in space were few.

"Yeah, it sure would be nice to have you up here with me more often."

Jennifer's head dropped. "Danny…"

"Yeah, I know. We've been through this a million times. You couldn't give up your work at the lab any more than I could give up my life on the *Stargazer*," he pulled her to his side and tilted his head next to hers, joining her gaze into space, "but I can have my dreams too."

She relaxed into his grasp. "It's not perfect, but if it's the only way that I can have you, then I'll share you with the stars." She turned her face toward him, her lips inching closer as she spoke. "The time that I spend with you is better than a lifetime with anyone else." Their lips met, and it felt as natural and comfortable as it felt scintillating. They held each other closely, their eyes now closed to the beauty of the heavens, their souls basking on the beauty within.

The silence lasted only a few moments. "I'm detecting a fluctuation in the spacewarp field around the starfighter. They should be dropping to thruster speed in approximately forty-five seconds." Even Blake's mechanical voice was tinged with a hint of anxiety at the confrontation that lay ahead.

"What's our position?"

T.C. had left his station at tactical, and had taken over navigation while Danny took a breather. Tactical would not be needed until the battle was near. "We entered Teconean space about five minutes ago. The Imperial fleet is pretty active, probably at full military alert, but there's not much action in this sector. The nearest ships are still a half hour away at their best thruster speed." Danny slipped out of Jennifer's arms, and took his station. He could control navigation and pilot the *Stargazer* from the main command console. T.C. stepped away, and went back to the tactical station to check weapons status.

Danny strapped himself in. "Well, boys and girls, this is it."

T.C. fastened himself in to the chair at the tactical station. Although the *Stargazer* had originally been designed for a crew of three, with a third chair situated behind the main communication station, he and T.C. usually flew alone.

Communications could easily be routed to either of the other two control consoles, but for this trip he had left the comm station active, with Jennifer at the controls. She took her seat and braced for a confrontation in which she would only be a helpless observer. "Well, Blake, let's hope that these two space cowboys are as good as they say they are."

"Amen," responded the computer. Jennifer let a slight smile curl her tense lips.

"There!" cried Danny, pointing to the viewscreen. The starfighter was in plain view, having dropped out of spacewarp. He checked his nav panel. "We'll overtake it in three minutes." He calculated his approach, trying to time the drop out of spacewarp to occur at the last possible moment. He knew that they would be detected almost instantaneously once they engaged their thrusters. "Check your monitor, partner, and warm up that trigger finger. We'll only get one pass."

"On it." T.C.'s gaze was fixed on his tactical monitor, where a three-dimensional holographic image popped up out of the display. It depicted the sector of space that the starfighter was in; superimposed over it was the tactical approach that Danny had been working on for the past few days. The image showed a simulation of their approach, and the view that T.C. would have...briefly...of the starfighter at the moment that he would be aiming his weapons. "Perfect, Danny. If you can get us in that position, I can't miss."

Blake interrupted. "I certainly wish that you two would give me weapons control. The precise calculations that my matrix is capable of are surely more..."

"Shut up!" was the simultaneous cry. Even Jennifer joined in this time.

"Well, I was only trying..." Jennifer hit the comm panel, and disengaged Blake's voice.

"Sorry, Blake, but this is *really* a bad time."

Danny and T.C. looked at her incredulously. She looked back, and just shrugged her shoulders. She knew where her best chance for survival lay.

Danny was intent on his screen. "Four, three, two, one…"

The *Stargazer* lurched softly, as the spacewarp field generator was disengaged. They hesitated for a split second, and then lunged forward at top thruster speed, maneuvering quickly on the planned trajectory around the starfighter's stern, and circling back in obliquely from the starboard side. T.C. could feel every sway of the ship; it was like sitting in a well-worn saddle on your favorite horse. "Just…a…little…bit…NOW!" He engaged the torpedo, and they held their breath collectively as they watched it streak toward the Teconean vessel.

*   *   *   *   *   *   *   *

The Starscape Project

Now available from Padwolf Publishing

The secret of the future's past and the key to the past's future lies buried on the moon of the human outworld, Kennedy Prime.

"It's a fun, fast-paced story that takes you back to a simpler time. If you like larger-than-life do-no-wrong heroes in a universe where good and evil are as clear as black and white then look no further."

…Michael D. Pederson, Nth DEGREE

*   *   *   *   *   *   *   *

Order *The Starscape Project* today
at
www.Padwolf.com
www.Amazon.com

Visit www.BradAiken.com

About the Author

Brad Aiken is a physician practicing in Miami, Florida. Miami Metro Magazine has recognized him as one of South Florida's top physicians on several occasions. He has published numerous scientific articles and has presented to both professional and non-professional groups on a variety of topics. Dr. Aiken has been the recipient of the Navy Science Award, as well as science awards from the Army, the Air Force and NASA. His award winning short stories can be viewed at: www.BradAiken.com.

978-0-595-13548-6
0-595-13548-X

Printed in the United States
31464LVS00005B/247-270